WHO'S GOT A CRUSH ON ANDY?

THE GIRLS OF CANBY HALL

THE GIRLS OF CANBY HALL

WHO'S GOT A CRUSH ON ANDY?

EMILY CHASE

SCHOLASTIC INC.
New York Toronto London Auckland Sydney

ISBN 0-590-42149-2

12 11 10 9 8 7 6 5 4 3 2 1   9/8 0 1 2 3 4/9

Printed in the U.S.A.   01

First Scholastic printing, March 1989

CHAPTER ONE

"Well?" Jane Barrett looked up from her book and over at her roommate, Toby Houston. "Do you think it's here yet?"

"You asked me that exactly two seconds ago," Toby reminded her.

"Sorry." Jane sighed and ran her fingers through her long blonde hair. Feeling a tangle, she decided to brush it. She searched the top of her desk, which was crowded with two empty juice cartons, a pile of clean, unfolded laundry, a towel still damp from her shower, and even a few books. But no hairbrush.

Toby watched, grinning, as Jane got down on her knees and looked under her bed. In spite of her "proper" Boston upbringing, Jane was an unreformable slob. Their other roommate, Andrea Cord, was a neatness freak, and Toby was somewhere in between. It made life in Room 407 interesting, Toby thought — except on a day like today. Out-

1

side, the grounds of Canby Hall, a private girls' school in the town of Greenleaf, Massachusetts, were covered with a layer of dull gray snow, and the cloudy sky was promising more. An icy wind whistled around the corners of Baker House, one of three dormitories on campus, and the radiators were doing their usual feeble job of heating the rooms. In spite of this, most girls were staying inside. It was Saturday, but it just wasn't a day for frolicking in the snow. Unfortunately, there wasn't much to do inside but study, and that wasn't high on anybody's list of exciting things to do. Neither was waiting for the mail, but it was better than studying, which was why Jane kept asking Toby if she thought it had come yet.

As Jane scooted out from under the bed, hairbrush in hand, Toby laughed. "I just had a notion," she drawled in her Texas accent. "How 'bout if you clean up your side of the room?"

Jane's eyebrows lifted in surprise. "That's a very strange notion," she remarked. "Why would I want to do that?"

"To help pass the time," Toby said.

Jane looked at her messy desk and her rumpled bed, which, if it had been made up, would have been covered with an antique quilt in shades of blue matching the Persian rug that was now entirely hidden by the clothes she'd taken off the night before. "It *is* a mess," she admitted. "But it's my mess and I'm comfortable with it. Besides," she went on, "if I clean it up, what would I do then?"

Toby laughed again. "Don't worry, I have another notion that it wouldn't stay clean forever."

"True," Jane agreed, briskly pulling the brush through her hair. "So why bother in the first place?"

"I can't argue with that kind of logic," Toby said in amusement.

"Besides, cleaning up is so dull," Jane added. She surveyed the mess again and then shrugged. "Everything is kind of dull right now. I just can't seem to get interested."

Toby nodded. "Greenleaf isn't Montavia, that's for sure. And Baker House is a far cry from a castle."

Jane touched the radiator behind her desk. Stone cold. "A very far cry from a castle," she agreed and started searching for a sweater.

The two girls went back to their studies, both of them thinking of their recent trip to Montavia, a small country in Europe. Princess Allegra, who had visited Canby Hall the year before, had gotten married. And since she'd become good friends with all three roommates, she'd invited them to Montavia to the wedding and Andy was one of her bridesmaids. It had been a wonderful trip, the kind of thing that would probably happen only once in a lifetime, and after the glitter of the palace and the excitement of a royal wedding, the residents of 407 were finding life at Canby Hall almost as gray as the winter sky outside.

Toby stopped pretending to study history and stared up at the ceiling over her bed, her green eyes squinting thoughtfully at the tea bag she'd hung there when she first came to Canby Hall. "You know," she said after a few minutes, "there's another reason you might want to clean your side of the room."

"What?" Jane asked.

"It might cheer Andy up."

Both of them looked at Andy's part of the room, which was spotless, as usual, the desk dust-free and orderly, not a piece of clothing in sight, the bold, geometric-print bedspread unwrinkled and completely visible except where Andy's collection of stuffed animals sat. The whole area was so incredibly neat that it looked like no one had set foot in it for at least a week, which was almost true.

Coming back to Canby Hall had been a minor let-down for Jane and Toby, but for Andy, it had been more like a major crash. And it wasn't just that the "common" life in Greenleaf was so dull: Someone as outgoing and energetic as Andy could find excitement living in a hut. But Andy had fallen in love in Montavia, and it hadn't worked out. Depressed, Andy had even more energy than when she was happy. Andy was awake before Toby (whose upbringing on a Texas ranch made her rise at daybreak) and out of 407 long before Jane ever opened her eyes. She went to classes of course, but before, in between, and after, no one was quite sure what she did. The only thing she *didn't* do was talk about how she felt.

"Where is she, anyway?" Jane asked now.

"Dancing, probably," Toby said, twisting one of her bright red curls around a finger. "She spends a lot of time over at the theater. I know she wants to be a ballerina someday, but with all the practicing she's been doing since we got back, she'll be completely tuckered out by the time she gets the chance."

Jane nodded. Privately, she was relieved that Andy wasn't moping and crying and using up tons of tissues over her broken romance. Raised in a wealthy Boston household, Jane had been taught that extreme displays of emotion were unseemly, and she couldn't help being uncomfortable around them. But she was hardly comfortable with the way Andy was acting now, either. Andy was so busy keeping busy that she didn't have time for her two best friends. She never sat down and "chewed the fat" anymore, as Toby put it, and normally, Andy was a true chatterbox. But worst of all was the way she laughed. She *did* laugh, but there was a hollow ring to it, and her dark eyes never even crinkled at the corners.

Maybe Toby was right, Jane thought. Maybe cleaning the room *would* cheer Andy up. And if it didn't, at least it would surprise her.

"Okay," she said, putting her hairbrush down. "I'll do it. I'll clean this mess." She took the two empty juice cartons and tossed them into the wastepaper basket. "Of course," she added, "what I should really do is let *Andy* take care of it. That way she could keep busy and have a clean room at the same time. *That's* probably what would cheer her up."

While Jane was reluctantly tackling the mess in her area of the room, with Toby giving a hand and cheering her on, Andy was trying to decide what to do next. As Toby had guessed, she spent most of the morning in a rehearsal room, practicing at the barre until she felt ready to drop, then pushing herself to go on. But now she'd reached the point where she really couldn't go on. Much as she'd like to, she couldn't dance sixteen hours a day, so the problem now was how to fill the rest of the hours until she could flop into bed and sink into sleep.

A shower first, she thought. She stepped into a pair of sweatpants, checking the big clock on the wall. It was lunchtime — good.

Jane and Toby would be in the dining hall, griping about the food but eating anyway, because neither one of them had birdlike appetites. So Andy could shower, change, and be gone again before they got back to 407. The less she had to talk to anybody, the better, especially to Jane and Toby, because they cared so much.

At least they were leaving her alone, she thought, tugging on a yellow sweatshirt and zipping herself into her bright orange winter jacket. All she needed was to be left alone — and lots of things to do — and everything would work out fine.

Jamming an orange stocking cap on her head, Andy grabbed her duffel bag and hurried outside. The wind hit her hard as she rounded the corner of the theater building, but she marched right through it. Coming from Chicago, she was used to cold winter winds. Not that she was crazy about them, but she wasn't about to let them stop her.

The campus was almost empty, she noticed. What was the matter with everybody? Didn't they have anything better to do than sit inside like old people afraid to slip on the ice? She, for one, was much too busy to let the weather keep her from doing what she had to do.

The question was, after a shower, what *did* she have to do? She'd already danced till she was ready to drop, and there wouldn't be any rehearsals for the new program until Monday, and no new homework assignments until then, either. She could go ice skating. That always burned off a lot of energy. But by this afternoon, she knew that a lot of kids would want to escape the dorm in spite of the weather, and the rink would probably be crowded. She definitely didn't want a crowded place.

Striding briskly along a narrow path, Andy suddenly slipped on a patch of ice and found herself sprawled on a dirty pile of snow. Her duffel had gone flying, so Andy scrambled up and skidded down the snowpile after it.

The bag was lying just at the edge of the Wishing Pond, a small pool where girls made wishes and threw pennies (and sometimes quarters, hoping a bigger investment would help). Andy had tossed in a few pennies herself. She stared at the pond, which was now covered with a layer of ice, and without meaning to, she started remembering the trip to Montavia. And Ramad, the handsome prince from a North African principality, the young man she'd fallen in love with — so much in love that she was ready to give up her dream of becoming a dancer, ready to give up everything, marry him, and follow him back to his home.

Jane and Toby had tried to talk sense to her, of course, but she wouldn't listen. Finally, though, she'd had to listen. But not to her roommates. To Ramad. He was the one who'd realized that by marrying him and becoming his princess, she'd be giving up her freedom. And that it would break her spirit, which was what he loved most about her. So they'd ended things and she'd come back to Canby Hall.

Ramad was right, of course, Andy knew that. If she'd followed her heart, she'd be in a society where she couldn't dance, couldn't take a walk without a bodyguard, and where she certainly couldn't call up the local pizza place at nine o'clock at night and order a pie with extra cheese.

She'd felt lost when she first came back, but she was slowly getting over it. She still had her legs, so she could dance. And she still had her mind, which was pulling better grades than she'd ever gotten in her life. So she couldn't trust her heart anymore, so what?

Glancing at her watch, Andy discovered she'd been sitting by the pond for ten minutes. She shook her head, annoyed with herself. She had to get moving. Look what happened when she stopped — she started remembering, which was a complete waste of time.

"I *thought* that was you, Andrea Cord!" a voice called.

Andy slung her duffel bag over her shoulder, stood up, and turned to face Gigi Norton.

"Isn't it a little hard to make wishes when the pond's frozen?" Gigi asked, her bright red lips curving in a sarcastic smile. Jane's nickname for her was the Worst Person in the World. Andy wasn't sure about the world part, but Gigi was definitely the worst person at Canby Hall.

"Don't you know?" Andy asked, putting on an overbright smile. "The best time to wish is when it's frozen. That way, your penny doesn't sink and neither does your wish."

"Sure." Gigi rolled her eyes, although Andy wasn't sure how she managed it. She wore so much makeup, her eyelids probably weighed a pound apiece. "Well, I hope you weren't wishing for a perfect grade on our research paper in English," she went on. "Because I just checked out every book the library has on it." Hoisting her load of books, she gave Andy a satisfied smirk and then headed down the path.

Andy watched her for a few seconds, shaking her head. Look what else happens when you don't keep moving, she told herself. You run into people like Gigi Norton.

Actually, though, she decided that annoying as Gigi was, she'd done her a favor. Andy hadn't forgotten the research paper, but since it wasn't due for another month, she hadn't started it yet. Well, she'd start it today. It was too bad she and Gigi had picked the same subject — the plays of Eugene O'Neill. But if Gigi had cleaned out Canby Hall's library, that was no problem. Greenleaf had a perfectly good library of its own.

Now that she had something to do for the rest of the day — for the rest of the month, really — Andy felt on track again. No more looking back for her. The thing to do was keep moving forward. Eyes straight in front, she strode quickly back to Baker House, took a lightning-fast shower, dressed, and was on her way to the Greenleaf library while the girls in the dining hall were still trying to decide if the stuff on top of the Jell-o was whipped cream or cold cream.

"She was here," Jane announced as she walked into 407. "Look."

Toby looked to where Jane was pointing and saw a slight wrinkle in Andy's bedspread.

"That wrinkle wasn't here this morning," Jane said positively.

"Yep," Toby agreed. "She didn't cover her tracks so well this time."

The two of them had just come back from lunch. The mail had finally arrived, and they were eager to read their letters. But they were more eager to see if Andy — the old Andy, they hoped — might be there.

"She's been and gone," Toby sighed, sinking onto her bed.

"That sounds suspiciously like a country-western song," Jane remarked. Her favortite composer was Beethoven, and as far as she was concerned, country-western didn't qualify as music.

Toby ginned. "It is, but don't worry, I don't know the rest of it." She started to open the letter from her father and then stopped. "Maybe we should have brought Andy's care package up with us. It's been sitting downstairs since yesterday and whatever's in it might spoil."

Jane stopped scanning the letter from her sister Charlotte, who was in college. "I think we should leave it," she said. "It can be sort of a test. Once Andy brings it up, we'll know she's back to normal."

CHAPTER TWO

On Monday, Andy's care package was still sitting in the main hall of the dormitory, waiting to be picked up. Nobody had touched it, but everyone was dying to know what was in it. It might be homemade fudge, which was always a favorite, or cookies, cinnamon-raisin bread, an angel cake, or even a combination of several mouthwatering goodies. Not only was Andy's family large, loving, and determined to keep her supplied with treats from home, but her parents owned and ran a restaurant, which made their care packages the best in Baker House.

"I think it's a cake," Maggie Morrison from Room 409 said. She pushed her glasses up and took a closer look at the package. "Definitely. See how tall the box is?"

Dee Williams, Maggie's roommate, shook her head, her long blonde hair swinging across her shoulders. "I say it's cookies. Stacks of them."

"With that size package, it could be both," Penny Vanderark suggested hopefully in her southern accent. "Or maybe it's caramel corn. That takes up a lot of room."

The three of them, along with Jane and Toby, had just come back from morning classes and picked up their mail. It was time for lunch, but they were more interested in the food in Andy's package than the food in the dining hall.

"They sent caramel corn the last time," Jane reminded them. "And they never send the same thing twice in a row."

"Jane's right," Toby agreed. "It *is* a big box though. It has to be a cake or a combo."

They were all still staring at the package, as if by looking hard enough they might see through the brown paper and cardboard, when Meredith Pembroke, the dorm's housemother, walked by.

Merry stopped and watched them for a moment, then said, "It's not ticking, I hope."

Jane shook her head. "It's probably rotting," she said glumly.

"And there's nothing we can do about it," Maggie agreed.

Penny sighed. "Such a sad fate for such a sumptuous feast."

"Oh, I get it," Merry laughed. "This is a famous Cord Care Package, right?"

Dee nodded. "It's been here since Saturday."

"You mean Andy hasn't picked it up?" Merry asked in surprise. "What's the matter with her?"

The five girls exchanged glances. They all knew what the matter was with Andy, but they didn't feel right discussing it with the housemother, even one as understanding as Merry.

Finally Toby said, "She's just real busy. Maybe she didn't even notice it."

Merry nodded. "Well, why don't you take it up for her?" she asked.

Another look was exchanged. "We thought she should do the honors, since it's hers," Jane said lamely.

Slightly mystified, Merry nodded again. She hadn't missed those glances, but she decided not to pry. "Well, tell her about it," she suggested to Jane and Toby.

"We will," Jane said. "When we see her."

"*If* we see her," Toby muttered.

"Oh, I think you will," Merry said. "I just saw her outside. She was chatting with Ms. Allardyce, and now she's heading this way." With a smile, Merry crossed the main hall in three quick strides of her long legs, leaving the girls staring at each other again.

"She was chatting with P.A.?" Maggie said unbelievingly. "*Andy?*"

Patrice Allardyce, or P.A., as the students

privately called her, was Canby Hall's head-
mistress. Cool and aloof, she was not the
type of person Andy — or anyone — usually stopped to chat with.

"I hope she's not in trouble," Maggie said.

"She couldn't be," Jane said. "She's too
busy to get in trouble."

Just then, Andy came bounding into the
main hall, her long yellow muffler flying out
behind her. "Hey, great!" she said when she
saw the others. "I was hoping you'd be
around."

"*We're* usually around," Penny told her.
"You're the one who's turned into what my
momma calls a real gadabout."

"Right," Andy said, with one of her too-
hearty laughs. "Anyway, I was just over at
the Greenleaf library, and I saw all these
notices that Greenleaf High School's having
a winter carnival."

"My," Toby said dryly. "That's real interesting."

"For Greenleaf High School," Maggie
added.

"Which I didn't even know existed," Jane
said.

"Well, of course it exists," Peggy said.
"The question is, what does its winter carnival have to do with us?"

Everyone turned back to Andy, who by
now was tapping her foot impatiently. "It
doesn't have anything to do with us," she
said. "But it made me think — why

shouldn't Canby Hall have one, too? It would be great! So I told P.A. and she thought it was a great idea, too."

Andy finally took a breath, and Toby broke in. "What happens in a winter carnival?" she asked.

"Oh, you know, sled races, snowman-building contests, ice hockey. . . ."

"A snowball fight?" Maggie suggested.

"Sure, maybe between the three dorms," Andy said. "That would be wild! Listen," she went on, "I can't talk now, but we'll come up with some more ideas tomorrow night."

"We will?" Jane asked.

Andy was already heading for the stairs, peeling off her muffler on the way. "Right. Didn't I tell you? P.A. put me in charge of the whole thing, and I've decided all of you should be on the committee."

With that, Andy was gone.

"What!" Toby exclaimed. "No way!"

"I don't think you have a choice," Penny teased.

"Andy has spoken," Jane said dryly.

"Oh, is that who that was?" Dee joked. "She came and went so fast, I wasn't sure."

"We forgot to tell her about that," Maggie said, looking mournfully at the care package. "Now we'll have to wait another day to find out what's in it."

"Why don't we just carry it on up to 407 for her?" Penny suggested.

"Oh, no!" Jane cried, stepping in front of the package to block it. "This box doesn't budge until Andrea Cord is back to normal!" She thought a second, and then added, "Or until it starts to smell, whichever comes first."

Ten minutes later, Jane and Toby walked into the Greaf Diner and sat down at the counter. The place was really the Greenleaf Diner, but four of the letters on its sign had been missing for so long that no one ever called it by its original name. Once Jane had seen what the dining hall was serving — chicken chow mein — she'd talked Toby into going with her to the Greaf.

Toby didn't need much convincing. Her stomach could handle the dining hall's food, but her taste buds sometimes begged for mercy.

"Ladies, what a pleasant surprise!" Cary Slade said as he handed them each a menu and filled their water glasses. "What drove you out of the dining hall and into our humble establishment today?"

Toby laughed. She always enjoyed Cary, who was Jane's boyfriend. He went to Oakley Prep, a boys' school down the road from Canby Hall, and even though he had the same wealthy Boston upbringing as Jane, the two of them were completely different. Cary dressed "down," as he called it, wearing mostly jeans and sweatshirts, while Jane was as preppie as they came. Jane almost never did anything unless she'd thought about it for at least three days; Cary's middle name should have been spontaneous. But the two of them usually got along great, and even when they fought, Toby suspected they enjoyed it.

"Well?" Cary asked. "What was the dining hall trying to pass off as food today?"

"Chicken chow mein," Toby said.

"You mean chicken ptomaine," Jane corrected. "It's — "

"Spare me the description!" Cary clutched his stomach, his blue eyes squinting in fake pain. "I don't even want to imagine it."

"Imagine this then," Jane told him. "A large Coke, a double cheeseburger, and an order of onion rings."

"Imagine it twice," Toby said. "But with milk on the second one."

"Consider it done," Cary said, taking their menus and snapping them closed. "One question, though. Why did you let Andy stay and partake of the poisoned poultry?"

"Don't worry," Toby said. "She knows all about the chicken ptomaine — she's the one who named it."

"Besides," Jane added, "Andy doesn't stop long enough to actually sit down for her food these days — she's doing everything on the run."

After Cary went off to the kitchen, Jane

kept talking about Andy. "I know it was my idea to leave her alone," she said. "It just didn't seem like she wanted to talk or anything. But maybe it wasn't such a good idea. If I could get her to stop for five seconds, I'd try to talk to her."

"What would you say?" Toby asked, rummaging in her backpack.

Jane started to answer and then shook her head. "I don't really know. I can't talk about her moping, because she's not. I guess it would sound dumb if I complained that she's too busy."

Toby nodded, still pawing through her backpack.

"She smiles a lot, she laughs a lot, she hasn't stopped dancing or studying," Jane went on. "But you and I know that she's not happy. Don't we?"

"Yep," Toby muttered. "This dumb pack! Everything I want falls to the bottom."

"What are you looking for?" Jane asked in exasperation. "I can tell we're never going to get around to discussing Andy until you find it."

"My letters. I got two and they've both disappeared on me."

"Try your pocket," Jane said. "I saw you stick something in there."

Toby reached around to the back pocket of her jeans and pulled out the two letters. "Thanks," she said with a grin. "I should have remembered. I always keep the important stuff there."

"Speaking of important stuff," Jane said, forgetting Andy for the moment, "here comes lunch."

"*Voilà!*" Cary announced, setting their plates down with a flourish. "The finest burgers on either side of the Mississippi." He waited for Toby to disagree, but she was busy looking at her mail, so he turned to Jane. "This is your lucky day," he told her. "I just got a five-minute break. And I plan to spend all five of them with you."

Jane smiled as she doused her burger with ketchup. "That's what I love about you — you're so modest."

Cary laughed and leaned his elbows on the counter. "Hey, how about if we catch a movie tomorrow night? They're showing an old Beatles' film."

"That might be fun," Jane said doubtfully. Cary was a true rock fan; in fact, he played lead guitar in a group called Ambulance, and even though Jane admired his dedication, she couldn't quite understand it. "I have an awful lot of studying to do, though, and it *is* a school night. . . ."

"I said it's the Beatles," Cary reminded her, laughing again. "They were geniuses, but compared to what's going on today, they were very tame. Your ears will survive, I promise. And it starts at six, so you'll have plenty of time to hit the books afterward."

Jane was just about ready to agree when she remembered Andy's committee meeting. She wasn't sure she was interested in helping to plan a winter carnival, but she thought she ought to show up for at least the first meeting. "I can't," she said to Cary. "Not tomorrow night, anyway. Andy sort of commanded some of us to help her with this idea she had."

While Jane went on to tell Cary about the Winter Festival, Toby opened her first letter. The other one, from Neal Worthington, she decided to save. Cornelius Worthington III, better known as Neal, was from Boston, like Jane. In fact, he'd once been Jane's boyfriend, and the two of them were still good friends. But now there was something special between Neal and Toby. She still couldn't understand how a girl from Rio Verde, Texas and a boy from Boston's high society managed to hit it off so well, but they did. Maybe it was because they both laughed at the same things, or because they both loved the outdoors so much. Whatever it was, Toby was glad, and she knew Neal's letter would make her grin from ear to ear. So she set it aside, like dessert, and picked up the one from Texas.

This was the second letter she'd gotten from her father in three days, which was strange. Normally, they wrote to each other once a month. Toby couldn't remember her mother very well; she'd died when Toby was very young, but as far as wordiness went, Toby knew she took after her father. The two of them could go for days without saying much more than "mornin'" and "sleep tight." What could her father possibly have to say that couldn't have waited until his next turn to write?

Hoping that nothing was wrong, Toby ripped open the letter and read it quickly. Then she read it again, this time more slowly.

Dear October,
   I hear on the news that you're getting some real 'weather' up there in Mass.

Toby frowned. He'd said the same thing in his other letter.

   Forgot to mention that I went to the ranchers' meeting the other night. Everybody's hoping for a mild winter. Don't want to lose any cattle in a freak storm like last year.

What else is new? Toby wondered. The ranchers always hoped for a mild winter. He didn't have to write an extra letter to tell me that.

   Max is in good spirits. Still kickin' up his heels, even though he's gettin' old. Smart horse, I say. Enjoy life while you've got it, it goes by real fast.

Got to close. The Bargers expect me for supper. Sure am glad to have neighbors like them.

Love,
Dad

After reading the letter a third time, Toby stuffed it back in the envelope and put it away. But instead of opening the one from Neal, she put her chin in her hands and leaned her elbows on the counter, staring off into space.

There was something very strange about that letter. She couldn't put her finger on it, but it just didn't feel right. "Enjoy life while you've got it, it goes by real fast," her father had said. And he'd said something like it in his last letter — "Been real busy lately, but I like it. No sense in rockin' on the porch until I have to."

If her father was trying to tell her something, why didn't he just come right out and say it? Toby wondered. Maybe he can't, she thought, suddenly. Maybe it's too hard for him to say. But what could be so hard to talk about?

"Toby?" Jane's voice broke into her thoughts. "We've got classes in twenty minutes and your hamburger's getting colder by the second."

Toby blinked and looked at her untouched burger.

"What's wrong?" Jane asked.

"Just thinking," Toby said, giving herself a shake and reaching for the ketchup. She started to mention the letters and then decided not to. She was probably imagining things. If something was wrong, her father would tell her. Wouldn't he?

CHAPTER THREE

On Tuesday, right after dinner, Andy's Winter Festival Committee had its first meeting in Room 407. Since she had a paper due the next day, Dee had begged off, but Maggie, Penny, and Jane were there. Toby was late, but Andy decided to start without her.

"Toby probably just stopped to talk to somebody or brush the taste of dinner out of her mouth," Jane said. "Why don't we wait a few minutes?"

"Because I want to get over to the Greenleaf Library. It closes in forty-five minutes," Andy told her. Using her desk as a barre, she started doing some deep knee bends. "And then I have to put in some work on my piece for dance class. I don't have time to wait."

"You sure are the busy bee these days," Penny drawled, leaning back against Toby's bed. "Exercising your brain *and* your body. I get tired just watching you."

With a quick laugh, Andy handed her a pad and pen. "Since you want to be a writer, I thought you could take notes."

"My goodness, you're so organized, too!" Penny commented. She and Jane were about equals when it came to sloppiness.

Maggie yawned and then laughed. "Sorry. The radiators are working tonight, and it's so warm in here it makes me sleepy."

Andy did a couple of stretches and said, "Let's get started, okay?"

"Aye, aye!" Penny flipped open the notepad. "I'm standing by, Captain."

Andy stopped exercising and started gathering her books and papers together. "Well, we already talked about a snowman — excuse me, snow-*person* building contest, an ice hockey game, a sled race, and a snowball fight. How about some other ideas?"

Jane stifled a yawn. "What if the snow doesn't last?" she asked.

"That would be great!" Penny sighed. Then, seeing the look on Andy's face, she giggled. "But not for a winter festival, of course."

"We could sell hot apple cider," Andy suggested, checking the due date on a library book.

"That sounds great," Maggie said. "I'd love some right now."

"And something to eat with it," Jane added. She looked at Andy. "Like fudge."

"Or cake," Maggie said.

"Homemade, of course," Penny put in. "Hint, hint."

But Andy was feeling slightly annoyed at the way everybody kept getting off the subject of the carnival, and didn't take the hint about her care package. "I've got to go now," she said, slinging her duffel bag over her shoulder. She walked to the door and then stopped. "Maybe the rest of you can come up with some more ideas while I'm gone. That way this meeting won't have been a total waste."

"Uh-oh," Penny said after Andy left. "We made her mad."

"Well, we weren't much help," Maggie admitted. "We didn't contribute a single idea. And she did say she didn't have much time."

"Nobody's forcing her to be so busy," Jane pointed out. "She's the one who decided to be Super Girl."

"That poor thing's going to wear herself to the bone tryin' to get over the prince," Penny said.

"She's going to wear *us* to the bone, too." Jane got up and stretched, then looked at her watch and frowned. "I could have been at the movies with Cary right now," she said wistfully.

"Don't let Andy hear you say that," Maggie told her. "I have a feeling she'd hit the ceiling."

"Or me," Jane joked. "Come on, I guess we'd better try to brainstorm some ideas about this festival." She tried to think of something to add to Andy's list of ideas, but her mind just didn't seem to be working. It *was* awfully warm in the room for once; maybe that was it. Or maybe it was her stomach. Dessert had been lumpy lemon pudding and after one bite, Jane had decided her sweet tooth was just going to have to suffer tonight. Of course, there was always the vending machine downstairs. "Is anybody else hungry?" she asked.

"We all go to Canby Hall, don't we?" Penny said, as if the answer should be obvious.

"Then let's take a walk downstairs," Jane suggested. "I always think better when my stomach's happy."

"Let's just avoid looking at Andy's care package," Maggie said, as they all got up to leave. "I can't believe she still hasn't opened it. Every time I pass by, my mouth starts watering. I don't know how much longer I can stand it."

"You've just got to grit your teeth and think of something else," Jane said. "I know it's hard, but the only way we'll know Andy is back to normal is when she brings that package up here to 407 and opens it up of her own free will!"

While Jane, Penny, and Maggie were treating themselves to stale candy bars from the vending machine, and trying not to compare them to whatever might be in the unopened box in the main hall, Andy was walking quickly down Greenleaf's main street toward the library. The air was so cold it made her eyes water and her nose run, but she was so mad she hardly noticed.

Why had she bothered asking them to help her with the festival, anyway? They weren't interested. Dee, as usual, left a paper to finish at the last minute, and Toby didn't even show up. And the others couldn't keep their minds on the idea long enough to be any help at all. All they wanted to do was talk and laugh and waste time. She was disappointed in them all, but mostly in Jane and Toby. Her two best friends, and she couldn't even count on them.

Well, she'd just do it by herself, then, she thought, pushing open the door to the library. It wouldn't be as easy, but at least it would get done.

Andy stamped the snow off her sneakers, unwound her muffler, stuck her gloves in her jacket pocket, and headed for the stacks. When she'd been there before, one of the books she'd wanted was out, and she was hoping it was back now. She was surprised it had been gone in the first place. As far as she knew, she and Gigi were the only ones who had picked Eugene O'Neill for their subject.

The book still wasn't there, though, at least not on the shelf. She checked all the books around where it should have been, just in case it had been put back wrong, but she still couldn't find it. As she was standing there, frustrated, she saw a boy wheeling a cart of books by the end of the aisle.

"Excuse me," she said, hurrying over to him, "Do you mind if I go through the books on this cart? Maybe the one I'm looking for is here."

The boy stared at her for a second, but Andy was already shuffling through the books. "I don't get it," she muttered, "did Eugene O'Neill become a hot topic all of a sudden?"

"What's the name?" the boy asked, trying to keep the books from sliding off the cart.

"Andy," she murmured. "Andy Cord."

"Not your name," he said. "The name of the book."

"Oh." Andy bent down to the cart's bottom shelf. "It's a long one and I never can remember. Here." She pulled a slip of paper out of her jacket pocket and handed it up to him.

He studied the paper for a second, then

handed it back. "This is a three-day book," he said. "I'll go see when it was checked out."

He was back in a few minutes, shaking his head. "Sorry. Somebody took it out yesterday. It'll be back the day after tomorrow. You can reserve it if you want to."

"Thanks, but I'll just come back, I guess," Andy told him, looking at her watch. "I'm in kind of a hurry right now." She started to go, and then looked at the cart. "I really made a mess of this didn't I?" she asked, trying to put the books back in order.

"Yeah, you really did," he agreed.

For the first time since she'd spoken to him, Andy stopped long enough to give him a close look. Was he joking or was he really annoyed about the cart? There was a gleam in his dark eyes, but he wasn't smiling. Well, she didn't have time to figure it out.

"I'm sorry," she said again, picking up another book and trying to figure out where it had been. "I'm not usually so messy. It's just that I'm in a hurry."

"I can see that." He put out his hand and took the book from her. "Let me do it. That's what they pay me for."

Andy didn't need to be told twice. She thanked him, hitched her bag up over her shoulder, and strode quickly out the door.

The boy watched her until she was out of sight, the gleam still in his eyes.

*   *   *

As Andy was heading for the theater building, and Jane, Penny, and Maggie were back in 407, finally talking seriously about the winter festival, Toby was sitting in one of the study rooms downstairs in Baker House. The study rooms were small and private, just right for one or two girls who had trouble concentrating in their bedrooms, or who didn't want to keep their roommates awake if they had to study late.

Toby had never used one, and when she'd first sat down at the desk, she decided she'd never use one again. It didn't have a window, and she needed a glimpse of the outdoors or she tended to get cabin fever and couldn't learn a thing. But tonight, Toby needed privacy, and for that, the room was perfect.

In front of her, spread out on the desktop, were three letters from her father. The third one had arrived that afternoon, and she still couldn't believe that a man of so few words had written three letters in four days.

The third letter was pretty much the same as the other two. He mentioned Max and the weather and wondered whether he should start on mending the corral fence now or wait and do the whole thing in the spring. Then he said that even though spring had always been his favorite time of year, he'd decided not to hibernate this winter, like he usually did. "No sense in wasting a whole season waiting for the next one to come along," was how he put it.

No sense at all, Toby agreed. But why on earth was her father even talking like that? There was no doubt in her mind — he was trying to tell her something. But what? What could have happened — or was going to happen — to make him talk about the seasons and about life being too short to waste?

Sitting in the small, windowless room, her chin in her hands, Toby suddenly felt terrified. She couldn't stay there a second longer or she'd go much more than stir-crazy.

Toby gathered up the letters, and in two quick strides, she was at the door. Flinging it open, she found herself face to face with Andy.

"I didn't even get a chance to knock," Andy said, fumbling with her duffel bag and an armful of books. "I just came back from the theater. I didn't know you ever used these rooms. What's up? A big test?"

"No, I just . . . thought I'd check it out," Toby said, stepping into the hallway. "You can use it if you want."

Toby obviously had something on her mind, but Andy didn't seem to notice. "I thought you'd be at the committee meeting tonight," she said.

"Committee?" Toby looked confused. "What committee?"

"The Winter Festival, remember? P.A. put me in charge of it, and I'll do it alone if I have to. But I really could use some help." Andy had decided that maybe she'd been a little unfair, thinking that Jane and Toby didn't care. After all, it had been her idea and she'd just sort of sprung it on them. They really did deserve another chance. Besides, if she got mad, *they'd* get mad, and then nothing would get done.

But Toby had something else on her mind besides a committee meeting, and she barely heard a word Andy said. "Sorry," she muttered, heading down the hall. "Got a phone call to make. You can tell me what happened later, okay?"

So much for that, Andy thought, watching her go. Now who was being unfair?

The rooms in Canby Hall's dormitories had telephones; unfortunately, they could only be used for incoming calls. To call out, the students had to use the hall phones. Toby started with the first floor, and by the time she'd made her way up to the fourth, she felt desperate. Every one of them was tied up. Having decided to call home, she didn't want to wait while some other girl giggled with her boyfriend or discussed a homework assignment with somebody from another dorm.

Standing on the fourth floor hallway, she

tried to decide what to do. She could ask to use Merry's, of course, but that was for emergencies. And even though Toby believed she had one on her hands, she didn't want to have to explain it. Not yet. Not until she knew for sure.

"You're kidding!" the girl on the phone said. "What happened next?" She was facing the wall and didn't see Toby standing there. "Really?"

Toby edged a little closer so the girl would see her and maybe take the hint.

"I don't believe it!" The girl shrieked with laughter. "She really said that? I don't believe it!"

I don't believe *this*, Toby though glumly. Should she interrupt or just go back to 407 and wait for half an hour? She was still trying to make up her mind when Jane came out of Penny's room down the hall.

"There you are," Jane said, catching sight of Toby and walking toward her. "I was wondering where you'd been. Have you seen Andy?" she went on. "I think she was a little upset with us — we weren't much help on the Winter Festival, but after a couple of candy bars, we . . ." Jane broke off, having gotten close enough to see the look on Toby's face.

"Toby?" she said. "What's the matter?"

Toby started to answer that nothing was, but then she changed her mind. She was a terrible liar; Jane would see right through her, and besides, she had to tell somebody or she'd burst.

"Nothing's the matter with me," she told Jane. "But I think . . . I'm afraid my father's sick. And I don't mean a cold. I mean really sick."

CHAPTER FOUR

Y ou see?" Toby said to Jane. "You see all that stuff about enjoying life while you have the chance and not sitting in rocking chairs until you've got to? What in tarnation would he say that for if something wasn't wrong?"

Jane bit back a smile. Toby's Texas expressions really took over when she was upset.

The two of them were in 407, and Jane had just finished reading Toby's father's letters, twice. She wasn't sure what to make of them. She had to agree that they didn't sound quite like the Mr. Houston she'd met when she and Andy had visited the ranch. He wasn't the type to use homespun expressions like the ones in the letters, even though he *looked* like the type. But that didn't mean he was sick. Maybe he'd just been thinking a lot or something. People change, after all.

"You know Dad," Toby said. "He's about

as talkative as a rock, even about piddly little things. So with something big and important, he'd have even more trouble finding the words." She'd been sitting on her bed with her back against the wall, the horse blanket she'd brought from home tucked behind her. But now she scooted to the edge, sat up straight, and took a tense breath. "I really think he's sick," she said.

"Now, wait a minute," Jane told her. "It doesn't have to be that at all."

"What else could it be?" Toby asked. " 'Life's short, enjoy it while you can'? People just don't think like that when everything's fine. It's when things go wrong that they start philosophizing."

"But he doesn't have to be talking about illness," Jane argued. "A bunch of cows might have gotten lost or maybe a fence blew over during one of those famous Texas 'breezes.' "

Toby flopped back on her bed, sighing. "He would have told me about that stuff, Jane."

"I guess you're right," Jane admitted. "But if somebody's sick, it doesn't have to be him. Remember the time he wrote about Max and his cough? You thought it was your horse, and it turned out to be your uncle."

"I remember." Toby couldn't help smiling a little. "But it's not Max this time. He said he was in fine spirits."

"I know, but maybe it's a friend. It could even be these neighbors. . . ." Jane picked up one of the letters and scanned it.

"I already thought of that," Toby said, staring at her tea bag as if it might have the answer. Jane suddenly wondered if that's what the bag was — a sort of Texas crystal ball. Toby had never told anyone why she'd put it there or what it meant.

But Toby didn't mention the tea bag. "He'd tell me if somebody *else* was sick," she went on. "Besides, the Bargers invited him to dinner, and that's really weird."

"What's weird about it?" Jane asked. "My parents go to friends' for dinner or have friends over all the time."

Toby smiled again. "I bet they wouldn't if their friends lived twenty miles away over a dirt road as bumpy as an old-fashioned washboard. Besides," she added, "my father's a good neighbor, and he's not unfriendly, but he's just not the social type. Everybody knows it. The Bargers are always inviting him over and he almost never goes. But they wouldn't take no for an answer if they knew he was sick. Mrs. Barger's a great cook and she thinks the right food can cure anything."

"Why would he tell them and not you?" Jane asked. "That doesn't make sense."

"I don't know," Toby shook her head. "Maybe it slipped out. Or maybe he just can't figure out a way to tell me, so he's giving me these hints."

Jane put down the letter and stood up. "Then call him," she said, walking over to Toby's bed. "When you thought Max was sick, you were scared to call. But this is your father you're worried about, not a horse. So call him."

"I already tried. All the phones were tied up."

"And you let that stop you?" Jane took Toby's hand and pulled her to her feet. "Come on. If the phones are still busy, *I'll* fix it." She held up a hand as Toby started to protest. "Don't worry. I'll think of some story, so you won't have to explain why you need to call." She pushed Toby ahead of her to the door.

As it turned out, the phone in the fourth floor hall was finally free, so Toby was able to call from there. Unfortunately, Mr. Houston wasn't home.

"What time is it there?" Jane asked when Toby hung up.

"One hour earlier — nine-thirty," Toby said. "He's almost always in by now."

"Almost isn't always," Jane said. "Call again in half an hour. Maybe he forgot to milk a cow."

Toby called in half an hour, and another half hour after that. There was still no answer, and by then, she was getting so

worried that she forgot to remind Jane that
nobody milked cows at nine-thirty at night,
and even if they did, the ranch was a cattle
ranch, not a dairy farm.

Over the next couple of days, Toby tried
to call her father every chance she got. She
thought for sure she'd get him at his breakfast time, which was five-thirty in the morning, winter or summer, rain or shine. But
there was still no answer, and as she listened,
she imagined the phone ringing in the
empty kitchen at home, and got more and
more worried. Maybe her father was in
Lubbock, seeing a doctor. Or worse —
maybe he was in the hospital.

Jane urged her to call the neighbors who
had invited Mr. Houston to dinner, but
Toby didn't want to do that. If it was bad
news, she said, she wanted to get it straight
from the horse's mouth.

On Friday morning, Toby woke suddenly, sitting straight up in bed. She blinked
at the early morning light filtering in
through Jane's white curtains and wondered what noise had jolted her awake.
Then she realized that there hadn't been
any noise — she'd just made up her mind,
that was all. She was sick and tired of
listening to the phone ring, and if she had
to spend another day imagining what might
be wrong with her father, she'd go plumb
crazy. So, she wasn't going to spend another
day imagining things.

Once she'd decided what she was going to do, Toby felt much better, It was only six in the morning — too early to start making arrangements, but she couldn't go back to sleep. She'd take a walk, that's what she'd do. And by the time she got back, she could get the ball rolling.

Toby eased herself out of bed, being as quiet as possible so she wouldn't wake Andy, who was a light sleeper. She tiptoed over to the window to see what kind of day it was. No wonder it seemed bright — it was snowing again. Fat, wet flakes were spinning down like a shower of soap powder.

Hoping the weather wouldn't mess up her plans, Toby went quietly to the closet and took out her jeans. She pulled them on, then her cowboy boots, and started to inch open a drawer in her bureau, trying to find her thick, rust-colored turtleneck. The drawer stuck, as usual, and Toby gave it what she thought was a gentle tug.

The tug wasn't gentle enough. The drawer slid open, with a loud squeak, and Andy's head immediately popped up.

"I wasn't planning on getting up until seven," she said.

"Sorry," Toby whispered. She found the sweater and put it on. "I'll be out of here in a second."

"Is it snowing?" Andy squinted at the window. "It *is* snowing. What are you going out for?"

"A walk." Toby took her parka off the back of her desk chair. "I need some fresh air to get my mind working."

"Good idea." Andy yawned and sat all the way up. "Once it's working, maybe you can think about the Winter Festival."

"I'll try, but don't expect much," Toby said.

"Why not?" Getting out of bed, Andy quickly touched her toes a couple of times, and then looked at Toby. "Jane and Maggie and Penny finally came up with ideas about it. You can, too."

"Not today."

"Why not?" Andy asked again. "You always said you get a lot of good thinking done on these early-morning walks. All I'm asking is for you to spend five minutes of that thinking of the festival." She curved one arm over her head and bent to the side. "I don't see why you're making such a big deal about not doing it."

Toby was already at the door, but at Andy's last words, she stopped and turned around. "If you weren't so busy running around like a chicken with its head off, you might have found out what the big deal is," she snapped. "I've got other things on my mind, but if you're so desperate for ideas, here's one — why don't you just take the winter festival and — and cancel it?"

When Toby had gone, Andy slowly straightened up and then sat down on her bed. "What was that all about?" she wondered out loud.

"I can tell you." Jane raised herself on one elbow and propped her head in her hand. "If you really want to know."

"You're awake?" Andy asked in surprise. Jane would have been happy if classes started at noon.

"I know it's strange," Jane said with a yawn. "But the tension in this room was pretty loud, if you know what I mean." Yawning again, she sat up crosslegged on the bed. "Anyway, do you really want me to tell you what it was all about?"

"Sure I do," Andy said. "When somebody bites my head off for no good reason, I'd like to hear why."

"It was for a pretty good reason, actually," Jane said. Then she told Andy what was bothering Toby.

When Jane finished talking, Andy slowly shook her head. "Me and my big mouth. I can see why she was mad," she admitted. "But why hasn't she told me about it?"

"You know Toby," Jane said. "If she says 'I'm tired,' it's a major confession. She just doesn't talk about what's bothering her. And you have to admit," she added quietly, "you *have* been awfully busy lately."

Andy nodded and jumped to her feet. "Where do you think she went?" she asked, reaching for her bathrobe.

Jane fumbled on the floor and found her

alarm clock, looking shocked when she saw how early it was. "They're not even serving breakfast yet," she said, amazed that she was actually awake at six-thirty in the morning. "She probably went for one of her walks. Where are *you* going?"

"After her. To apologize."

Jane smiled. At least Andy wasn't too busy to stop and care. "You can't track Toby down, not even in the snow."

"But I want to apologize," Andy said. "And I might not see her again until tonight."

"Sure you will." Jane smiled again. "You'll see her at breakfast. No matter what the problem, Toby never misses chow time, remember?"

Andy hadn't been planning to eat breakfast. Not the dining hall's version of that meal, anyway. But she felt bad enough about what she'd said to Toby to give up her plans for a morning workout, followed by juice and a muffin from the Greaf, and take her chances on whatever was being served.

"Stick to the toast," Jane advised her, giving the poached eggs a suspicious glance. "Those things look like rubber."

"They *are* rubber," Andy said with a laugh. "That way, they're guaranteed to stick to your ribs."

Both girls by-passed the bacon, too, on the theory that it was underdone and might squeal when they bit into it. As soon as they sat down, they saw Toby take a tray and get into line.

"See?" Jane said, waving to their roommate. "I knew her stomach wouldn't let us down."

Toby waved back and joined them in a couple of minutes. Her cheeks were still pink from her walk, and her tray was loaded with everything the cafeteria had to offer, including a bowl of oatmeal.

"I know walking gives you an appetite," Jane said, looking at the tray in horror. "But it's supposed to give you an appetite for *food*, remember?"

Toby sprinkled sugar on her cereal and smiled. "Got to eat," she said simply.

Andy noticed the smile. What had cheered Toby up so fast? "Listen," she said. "I'm sorry about what happened this morning. Jane told me about your father and I—"

"It's all right," Toby broke in. "I didn't mean it about the festival, either."

"You look almost cheerful," Jane said eagerly. "What happened? Did you reach your father?"

Toby shook her head. "Nope. I just made up my mind, that's all." She smiled again. "I'm going home."

CHAPTER FIVE

I t's the only thing to do," Toby said flatly. "I can't hang around here another day, wondering what's wrong. I'm going home to find out."

Breakfast was over, but classes hadn't started yet, and the three roommates were back in 407.

"Don't try to talk me out of it," Toby went on, opening the closet door to get her suitcase. "I've already decided, and I'm not going to change my mind."

Jane and Andy had both been surprised at Toby's decision, but neither one of them wanted to change her mind. She could be as stubborn as a mule, for one thing, and for another, they didn't think it was such a bad idea.

"We're not about to try to talk you out of it," Andy said. "What we want to know are the details."

"Details?" Toby poked her head back out of the closet. "What do you mean?"

"Like when you're leaving, how you're getting there, have you gotten permission," Jane said. "Little things like that."

"Oh." Toby dragged out her battered suitcase and heaved it onto her bed. Then she sat down beside it. "I'm leaving today, after classes. And I have to call the airport in Boston to see if there's a plane out then." She smiled ruefully. "That's about as much as I've figured out."

Andy shook her head. "I'll tell you what," she said briskly. "You pack and get permission. We can't do that for you. But we'll take care of the rest. Right, Jane?"

"Right." This has made Andy's day, Jane thought. Now she's got another project to take her mind off Ramad. Well, at least this project has a good cause. Jane started searching the top of her desk, which hadn't stayed clean for long. "I think I've got Logan Airport's number in my address book," she said. "If I can find my address book."

"Wait," Andy said. "Calling the airport's one thing. But how's she going to get to the airport once she gets to Boston? And how's she going to get to Boston?" She took a deep breath. "Let's be organized about this."

Jane was right — Andy was definitely happy with the new project. She decided that Neal Worthington would organize things from his end in Boston — and she told Toby to call him before she did anything else.

While Toby did that, Andy used the third-floor phone to get the train and bus schedules from Greenleaf to Boston, and Jane called the Greaf to ask Cary to drive them to the train or bus, whichever one it would turn out to be.

"It'll be a pleasure," Cary told her. "Just name the time."

"I don't know yet," Jane said. "As soon as classes are over, I hope. Just be ready to roll."

"And rock?" Cary joked.

"Just roll," Jane laughed. She gave him a quick good-bye and raced off to class.

By lunchtime, everything seemed set. Neal reported that there was a plane to Lubbock at six-thirty. The train from Greenleaf got to Boston at five-fifteen, and he'd be waiting. He'd also bought the plane ticket.

"Uh-oh," Toby said, as she hung up the phone. "I forgot something."

"Impossible," Andy declared, checking her list. "Schedules, packing, transportation, you're about ready to talk to Merry . . . what's missing?"

"Money," Toby told her. "I forgot how much all this is going to cost."

Jane and Andy exchanged a glance. "We didn't forget," Jane said. She took an envelope out of her purse and handed it to Toby. "We pooled our money, and this will cover the plane ticket."

"We figured you had enough for the train," Andy added.

"I have more than that," Toby said, shaking her head at the envelope. They were being so generous, she felt tears stinging her eyes, and she started blinking furiously. "You're giving me too much."

"Take it anyway," Jane told her. "You might need it, and if you don't, you can give it back." She pushed the envelope into Toby's hand. "Better safe than sorry, I always say."

"Really?" Andy teased her. "I never heard you say that in my life."

"Well, somebody always says it," Jane replied with a laugh.

Their joking gave Toby a chance to blink back her tears, and she managed to laugh with them. "This somebody says thanks," she told them. "Thanks a whole lot."

For the first time since they'd returned from Europe, the three of them felt like a team. They went off to talk to Merry.

They were counting on Merry to be sympathetic and supportive, and she didn't let them down. As soon as she heard the story, she was on the phone to Ms. Allardyce, explaining the situation. Ten minutes later, Toby had permission to fly home.

* * *

"Here we are, ladies," Cary announced as he pulled the car up to the train station. "The Greenleaf-Boston Express." He looked at his watch. "And, I might add, I got you here with several minutes to spare."

"Which is a miracle, considering this car," Jane said. "Where did you get a bucket like this, anyway?"

"Bucket?" Cary pretended to be insulted. "I go from room to room, begging for any means of transportation at all, and when I finally get it, you call it a bucket?"

Andy got out and took a close look at the car. It was small, rusty, and at least twenty years old. "Jane's right," she agreed. "This isn't a car. This is a lemon on wheels."

With Cary grumbling about ingratitude, they went into the station, bought Toby's ticket, and then sat on a bench to wait for the train.

"Do you have everything?" Andy asked, checking her list again.

Toby nodded. "Suitcase, train ticket, chocolate truffles" — she smiled at Jane, — "and money. Neal's got the plane ticket, and that's all, right?"

"Wrong." Cary brought a hand out from behind his back and gave Toby a single red rose.

"Where did you get that?" Jane asked, impressed.

"There was a whole vaseful on the reception desk in my dorm," Cary said. "I didn't think one would be missed, especially in a situation like this. It's supposed to bring good luck, you know."

"It is?" Andy reached into her jacket pocket and took something out. "I thought this was." She opened her hand and held out a tea bag to Toby. "Actually, I don't know what it's for. But I thought it must mean something, so I got you another one to take with you."

Toby took it and stuffed it in her pocket. "Candy, a flower, and a tea bag," she said, starting to blink hard again. "I should leave more often."

Jane's throat felt tight, and she was afraid she might cry, something she never did in public. Fortunately, the train whistle sounded, and she used the noise to cover a loud sniff.

With another piercing whistle and a screech of metal, the train pulled into the station. Suitcase in hand, Toby stood up.

"Well, I'm off," she said.

Cary kissed her on the cheek. "That rose is for hope, too," he whispered.

"Don't forget," Andy reminded her, giving her a hug, "you've got to get a schedule for return flights, so we'll know when to meet you."

Jane hugged her, too. "Call the minute you can," she said. "No matter what."

"I'm not real thrilled about why I'm going," Toby said, managing to give them all one of her biggest grins. "But I sure can't complain about the send-off."

The train didn't sit long in Greenleaf, and almost as soon as Toby was on board, the whistle shrieked again. Five minutes later, the tracks were empty.

No one said much on the drive back to Canby Hall. Jane didn't know what the others were thinking, but in spite of her worry about Mr. Houston, and what it would mean to Toby if he really were sick, she couldn't help feeling good. Andy had not only taken charge of the entire getaway, but she'd stopped organizing things long enough to think about Toby's feelings and buy her a tea bag. Maybe the real Andy was starting to come back.

"I wish I could hang around for a while," Cary said, as he pulled the car up to Baker House. "But I've got a rehearsal with Ambulance and a physics test to study for." He kissed Jane and grinned at Andy. "Just let me know when Toby's coming back, and I'll try to borrow this lemon again."

Back in 407, Jane threw her jacket on her desk and herself on the bed. "What a day!" she said. "I feel like I've been moving furniture."

"I know," Andy said. "It's a real let-down when the adrenaline stops pumping."

Jane dragged herself into a sitting position, but her eyes were still closed. "When do you think Toby might call?"

Andy laughed. "She's not even airborne yet." She opened a drawer and took out a fresh leotard, some legwarmers, and her ballet shoes, and started putting them in her bag.

Jane's eyes opened a crack. "You're not," she said. "You're not really going to dance now, are you?"

"Not now. First I'm going to the library," Andy said. "There's a book I want. It's not supposed to be back until tomorrow, but I thought I'd check anyway." She zipped up the bag and headed for the door. "Then I'm going to dance."

"What about dinner?" Jane said quickly. "You can't run around all night without some food in your stomach."

"You sound like my parents," Andy told her. "I'll get something at the Greaf, or I'll buy a slice of pizza."

She put her hand on the doorknob, but Jane's voice stopped her again. "What about the winter festival?" Jane asked. "Shouldn't we be working on that?"

"I won't be that late — we'll have plenty of time when I get back."

"I was sort of hoping we could talk," Jane said, finally coming to the point.

"Maybe later," Andy said, not even asking what Jane wanted to talk about. "I've really got to go right now. The rehearsal room is really booked these days and if I don't show up, I'll lose my time."

Andy was halfway through the door when Jane called out, "That was a really nice thing you did — giving that tea bag to Toby. I could tell it made her awfully happy."

"Well, what are friends for?" Andy gave Jane a fast wave, an even faster smile, and then she was gone.

Good question, Jane thought, lying back on her bed. What *are* friends for? The way the three of them had come together today to help Toby had made her think that Andy was starting to get back on track. She'd been hoping the two of them would start talking about Toby's situation, and then move on to other things, mainly Andy's situation. But in spite of the tea bag, Andy hadn't changed. It was as if she'd scheduled the whole thing — "call train station, buy ticket, do something nice for Toby."

Well, it *had* been nice, Jane couldn't complain about that. But there was something missing. She couldn't quite put her finger on it, but it seemed that no matter how many things Andy did these days, her heart wasn't in any of them.

When the pilot told everyone to fasten their seat belts for the descent into Lubbock, Toby peered out the small window, hoping to see something familiar, which was silly, since it was dark outside. Not only could she not see a familiar sight, but when she got off the plane, she wasn't going to see a familiar face, either.

For the first time since she left that morning, she began to wonder if this had been such a good idea. She'd left Greenleaf like a bull out of the chute, and nobody here even knew she was coming. And it wasn't as if she could pick up her bag and walk home. The ranch was a four-hour drive out of Lubbock.

Well, she'd done it, and there was no turning back now. She just had to hope that her father was home, for once. And if he wasn't, then she'd just park herself here and keep dialing everybody she knew until she tracked him down. The one thing she wouldn't do was go back to school until she found out what was going on at home.

It didn't take long to find a bank of pay phones, and after buying a magazine and a package of gum with a twenty-dollar bill, Toby had enough change to keep the line tied up for quite a while.

Taking a deep breath, she shoved the coins into the slot and punched the number out at the ranch. She held her breath through seven rings, and was trying to decide whether to pass out or hang up, when the phone was answered.

"Hello?"

Toby had never been so glad to hear her

father's deep, dry voice in her life. "Dad? It's me."

"October?" Mr. Houston sounded glad and worried at the same time. "What is it, Toby? Is everything all right?"

"I'm fine," Toby assured him.

"Well. That's good." He paused, waiting for her to say why she'd called.

Toby cleared her throat. After all the running around today, she hadn't stopped to think about what she'd say. Finally, she laughed. "I see you're havin' winter out here, too. Forty degrees is pretty cold for these parts."

"You mean you've been listenin' to the weather?" Mr. Houston chuckled. "Thought you'd be too busy with your books for that."

"Well" — Toby took another deep breath. — "I didn't need to listen to the weather, because I can see it from where I'm standing," she said. "Get ready, Dad. I'm here."

"Here?"

"In Lubbock," Toby said. "At the airport. I got in about twenty minutes ago."

"You're in . . . well, what?" Mr. Houston was obviously very confused. "Toby, are you sure everything's all right?"

"No. I mean, *I'm* all right," Toby said quickly. "But I've been real afraid that you're not." She went on to explain how worried she'd been, how his letters had seemed strange, and how, after she couldn't reach him, she'd decided to come home.

When she finished, Mr. Houston didn't say anything for almost a minute. The operator came on and Toby put in more change, and then she waited for her father to talk.

"Toby? Well . . . my goodness, you sure have thrown me for a loop," he finally said. "You stay right where you are. Get yourself a bite to eat and I'll be over just as fast as I can."

"But Dad — "

"Now, I *do* have some news," he said. "But it's not anything to discuss on the telephone. Or in letters, for that matter." He chuckled again, then sighed, and Toby could picture him shaking his head. "Writing those letters was a dumb-fool thing for me to do. I never was any good at beating around the bush."

Toby got the feeling he was beating around the bush right then, and she wanted to tell him to get to the point, but he went on talking.

"You just sit tight, and when I get there, we'll get it all ironed out. Now let me get going, I don't want you spending the night at the airport." He paused a second, then said, "You did the right thing in coming, Toby. I'm glad you're here."

CHAPTER SIX

"Well?" Dee stuck her head around the door of 407 and grinned at Jane. "Has there been any action yet?"

Jane, who'd been half-heartedly studying her history notes, looked up from her desk in surprise. People almost never asked her questions about action, especially Dee, who teased her about being stuffy.

"What Dee means," Maggie said, joining her roommate in the doorway, "is did Andy break down and open her care package yet?"

"Oh. No," Jane told them. "The last time I saw it, it was still downstairs."

"And looking very lonely," Penny added, stopping in the doorway, too. "That poor box. I just hate to see something getting ignored like that."

"Face it," Dee laughed as Jane waved them into the room. "All we're really interested in is what's inside."

"You're right, we're awful," Penny agreed, sitting down on Toby's bed. "I suppose we should at least *try* to pretend we don't care, no matter how much our mouths are watering."

"But it's so annoying," Maggie complained. "I mean, she picks up her other mail. Why not that?"

"Can't you just ask her?" Dee said to Jane.

Jane shook her head. "I promised myself I wouldn't," she said. "It's Andy's package and I'm not about to beg her to open it."

"My, you sound as stubborn as Toby," Penny joked.

"Speaking of Toby," Maggie commented, "where is she, anyway? It's starting to snow pretty bad outside, even for one of her famous walks." Suddenly, Maggie's brown eyes brightened. "Wait! It *is* Friday night. Does she have a date?"

Jane shook her head again. With all the running around they'd done today to get Toby off, she'd forgotten to tell anyone else what was happening. "Toby's not here," she said.

"We can see that," Dee remarked dryly.

"No, I mean she's not in Greenleaf at all," Jane told her. "She's in Texas." Quickly, she explained about the letters from Toby's father, and how Toby had decided to go home and find out if anything was wrong. "It's eleven now," she said, checking her watch. "And they're an hour behind us, so

I guess it's too early for her to call. She wouldn't even be at the ranch yet."

"What do you think, Jane?" Maggie asked, looking worried. "You know Toby's father, a little. Were his letters really that weird?"

"I'm just not sure," Jane said. "They didn't give me the feeling that he's sick, like Toby thinks. But they didn't sound like the Mr. Houston Andy and I met, either."

"How do you mean?" Dee asked.

"He didn't talk much, naturally, but when he did, he said what was on his mind," Jane explained. "And he obviously had something on his mind when he wrote those letters, but he kept it to himself." She thought about what she'd just said. "So the answer is yes, his letters *were* weird."

"It's a true mystery, that's for sure," Penny commented.

"What's a mystery?" Andy asked, coming into the room just in time to hear Penny. She was still in her dancing clothes, her bag was slung over one shoulder, and her arms were full of books and papers.

"Have you been rehearsing all this time?" Jane asked.

"No, I came back a couple of hours ago, but I decided to use one of the study rooms for a while," Andy said. "Anyway, what's so mysterious?"

"Whatever's going on with Toby's father,"

Penny explained. "Jane just told us what happened."

Andy looked at the alarm clock by her bed. "Well, it's still too early," she said, dropping her books on her desk and peeling off her legwarmers. "Speaking of mysteries, I've got another one."

"A good one, I hope," Maggie said.

"It's not good *or* bad." Andy reached for her fluffy orange bathrobe and pulled it on. "Actually, it's kind of dumb."

"Well, what is it?" Penny asked.

For an answer, Andy reached into her duffel bag and pulled something out.

"A purple glove?" Dee asked. "What's mysterious about that?"

"This," Andy said, taking an envelope from among the papers and books she'd put on the desk. "I thought I'd lost one of these gloves, but look what I got in yesterday's mail." She opened the envelope and took out the matching glove, along with a piece of paper. "Dear Andy Cord," she read from the paper, " 'It's cold outside, there's snow and ice. You'll need this to keep your fingers warm and nice.' "

Jane cringed. "Is that supposed to be poetry?"

"Who cares?" Penny said. "The important thing is who sent it."

"That's the mystery," Andy said. "It's not signed. And," she went on, reaching into her bag and taking out another note, "neither was the one I got today."

"Two notes?" Maggie said. "This is getting interesting."

Andy carefully unfolded the note. " 'Dear Andy . . .' "

"Oh, it's *Andy* now!" Penny said. "How exciting!"

Andy smiled and went on, " 'Tomorrow night I'll see you dancing. Moving to music, you're sure to be doubly enchanting.' "

"You've got a secret admirer!" Penny cried. "And he's coming to the dance recital tomorrow night. He's going to be sitting out there in the darkened theater, worshiping you from afar! Now who could it possibly be?"

"Whoever it is, he's no poet," Jane said. Then she laughed. "But it *is* kind of romantic. Imagine somebody writing anonymous, admiring notes."

"Maybe it's Matt," Dee suggested, mentioning a boy from Oakley Prep that Andy dated from time to time.

Andy shook her head. "Matt's gone for two weeks on that student government trip, remember? Oh, well, at least I got my glove back." She shook her head at the notes and then dropped them in her wastepaper basket. "Now, since we're all here, how about working on the plans for the Winter Festival?"

The others looked at her in silent amazement.

"I simply do not believe you, Andrea Cord," Penny said at last. "If it were me, I'd be absolutely thrilled, not to mention dying of curiosity."

"Don't you even want to find out who it is?" Maggie asked.

"Not really," Andy said. "I mean, what difference does it make?" Reaching for a notebook and pen, she settled herself on the bed. "Okay, I ran into P.A. today and she grilled me about dates. So how soon do you think we can get the festival on the road? I thought maybe next Wednesday, since classes are going to be canceled for teachers' meetings."

As far as the others were concerned, the anonymous notes were a much more exciting topic of conversation. But they were Andy's notes, after all, and it was obvious that she wasn't the least bit excited by them. So with a collective sigh, they began to discuss the festival.

Jane, however, wasn't ready to give up on those notes yet. After the others left and Andy went off to shower, she took them out of the wastebasket. It couldn't be that hard to find out who'd sent them. Maybe she'd be able to find him at tomorrow night's dance recital.

True, he wasn't much of a poet, Jane

thought. But that didn't really matter. What mattered was that he seemed to care about Andy. And he was here, in Greenleaf, not in some North African principality half a world away.

Smiling, Jane stuffed the notes in her drawer and climbed into bed. He could be a real dud, of course. She'd have to meet him and talk to him. But if he turned out to be nice, then he just might be exactly what Andy needed.

It had been cold and windy when Toby first saddled Max for a ride early Saturday morning. Now, three hours later, it was still cold and windy. Toby's eyes were tearing and her fingers were stiff around the reins, but the last thing she wanted to do was leave the gusty plain and go back to the ranch.

Just ahead of her the ground sloped a bit — it couldn't really be called a hill, but it had enough of a slant to give her some protection from the wind. She rode over to it, slid off Max, and sat down on the hard-packed dirt. She had to think, and the only place she could do it was out here, no matter what the weather was like.

Of course, thinking was about the only thing she'd done since she'd gotten home last night. It had been late when she'd finally crawled into her bed, and after her father's news, all she'd wanted to do was sleep and forget about what he'd said. Instead, she'd tossed and turned and stared at the cracks in the ceiling until the sky outside changed from black to gray. Then she'd grabbed an apple for herself, a couple of carrots for Max, and headed outside.

Well, she thought, you've been turning things over in your mind for at least seven hours, and you still haven't figured out how you feel about them. You have to go back to the ranch soon, so you'd better do some fast figuring, right now.

One thing was certain — she was grateful. Her father wasn't sick. Far from it, as a matter of fact. When he'd walked into the airport last night, she knew from her first look that he was as well and happy as she'd ever seen him. There he was, his eyes sparkling, his smile wide, his arms reaching out to hug her.

And why was he so happy? Toby shook her head. Never in a million years would she have guessed it — her father was in love.

In love. Toby kicked at the dirt with the heel of her boot and shook her head again. That's where all that sappy talk about not spending the rest of his years rocking on the porch and enjoying life while he had it came from.

He wasn't just in love, though. That was only part of it. The rest of the news was that he was pretty sure he was going to "tie the knot." And even though he was tickled pink, he wasn't sure how Toby would feel about it, which was why his letters had been so strange. He hadn't figured out a way to say it, and he'd been trying to give her little hints.

"Of course," he chuckled, as he drove them home from the airport, "I guess all I did was give you a big scare."

That was the understatement of the year, Toby thought. She'd been terrified he was dying, and all the time he'd been "courting," as he put it.

Max, who'd been searching futilely for something to munch on, ambled over and nudged Toby in the shoulder. She looked at him. "Where were you while all this was going on?" she asked softly. "I leave you in charge for a few months and look what happens — Dad decides to get married again."

Max gave her another nudge, so she dug the second carrot out of her pocket and fed it to him. "How do you feel about this, Max?" she asked.

The horse didn't have any answers, of course. And when she finally climbed onto his back again, neither did Toby. But there was no escaping now — she had to go back to the ranch and meet the new love in her father's life. The only thing she was sure of, as she held Max to a slow trot, was that she was definitely not tickled pink about it.

* * *

"You'd think she would have called by now," Jane complained, looking at her watch. "It's ten o'clock there. She's probably been up for five hours, at least."

"She'll call when she's ready," Andy said for at least the tenth time. Then she looked out the window and frowned. Snow, again. At least a foot of it, and more coming down every minute. "I hope they don't have to cancel the recital tonight," she muttered, still staring outside. "I've been working like crazy for weeks."

Jane lay back on her bed. She'd planned to go to the library before lunch, but with all the snow, she'd decided not to. Maybe later she'd meet Cary and they could go sledding. "If they cancel it, they'll just re-schedule it," she said, getting into a comfortable position and reaching for a book. "I'm taking a few hours off. Why don't you?"

Andy turned and stared at her. "I've got a thousand things to do," she said. "I can't afford to be lazy."

Slowly, Jane closed her book and stared back at her roommate. "Well, I don't think relaxing for a little while means someone is lazy," she said, her voice clipped and cool.

"Okay, I'm sorry," Andy told her. "I didn't mean that. Just forget I said it."

But Jane didn't feel like forgetting it. "It might not be such a bad idea for you to relax for five minutes, too," she commented.

"What do you mean?" Andy asked. "I told you, I've got a thousand things to do."

"Oh, Andy!" Jane pushed her book aside and sat up. "When are you going to stop? Keeping busy isn't going to make you forget about Ramad."

Jane started to add that it was also driving the rest of them crazy, but when she saw the look on Andy's face, she bit the words back.

Andy's eyes were flashing and she looked like she might yell. Instead, she spoke very quietly, and Jane knew she was furious. "I'm not staying busy to forget about Ramad," she said, reaching for her jacket. "I've already forgotten about him. But if I keep busy, I'll make sure nothing like that ever happens again." Shrugging her jacket on, she grabbed her bag and walked out the door.

CHAPTER SEVEN

So," Jane said to Cary as they were walking to the dance recital that night, "now we know the problem — Andy's decided she's never going to fall in love again."

"There's a song somewhere in there," Cary remarked, stepping around an icy patch on the sidewalk. "In fact, I think somebody already wrote it. Too bad."

"This is serious," Jane told him.

"No, it's not. It's ridiculous." Cary laughed and took her hand. "You can't decide not to fall in love. It doesn't work that way."

"Try telling Andy that," Jane said.

"I would if I could get her to stand still long enough." Cary shook his head. "Boy, you were right about one thing — she's tearing around like crazy these days. When she used to stop by the Greaf, she'd take time to enjoy several minutes of witty con-

71

versation with me. Now, alas, she doesn't allow herself the pleasure."

"You mean she doesn't give *you* the pleasure of hearing yourself talk," Jane teased.

"I resent that," Cary said, not sounding the least bit resentful. "I don't deny it, but I resent it."

Jane squeezed his hand and laughed. "Well, anyway, I think I might have found a way to help Andy."

"Ah, you're going to sit her down and talk sense to her," Cary said. "Good idea."

"*I'm* not going to say a thing," Jane told him. She patted her purse where she'd put the notes from Andy's secret admirer. "I'm going to let somebody else do it."

"And who is this mystery person?" Cary asked.

"I don't know yet," Jane said. Then she told him about the notes. "So keep your eyes open tonight, and we just might find out."

Unfortunately for Jane, who was hoping to identify the mysterious note-writer, the weather hadn't kept many people from going to the dance recital, and the auditorium was packed.

"I thought this place would be half-empty," she said to Cary as they sidestepped their way to their seats. "It's going to be impossible to pick anybody out in this crowd."

Cary nodded. "I think there's a better way to solve this mystery," he said. "The guy returned her glove, right? So the thing to do is find out where she lost it."

"That could be anywhere," Jane told him. "She comes here to rehearse, she goes to classes, to the library, the Greaf . . . she's all over the place."

"But our mystery-man isn't," Cary pointed out. "He's only in one of those places, I'll bet. How else could he decide he likes her? Sure, a guy might see a girl once and think she's great. But if he never sees her again, what can he do?"

"That's right," Jane agreed. "He's in one place, where she goes a lot. And he's watched her. He's probably even talked to her. But either he's too shy to come right out and tell her he's interested in her, or else she's in too big a hurry to give him a chance. So he wrote the notes."

"Worshipping her from afar," Cary sighed.

Jane ignored him. "I'll just have to go where she goes and see if I can find a boy who looks like he's in love."

"Brilliant, Holmes."

"Thank you, Watson." Jane smiled as the lights dimmed and the curtain went up. This might be serious, but it could also turn out to be fun.

* * *

When Jane woke up the next morning, she was amazed to see that Andy was actually still asleep. Yawning widely, she fumbled for her clock. Nine-fifteen. An almost civilized hour to wake, as far as she was concerned, but she hadn't seen Andy sleep this late in weeks. But then, Andy had performed last night; she had to be tired.

Punching up her pillow, Jane got into a comfortable position and thought about the recital. As far as finding the note-writer went, of course, it had been a total loss. But she'd watched Andy more closely than usual when she was dancing, and she was convinced that she was right — Andy had shut her feelings off.

Oh, she'd danced beautifully, there was no question about that. All the dance students had performed solos of the routines they were working on, and they weren't even supposed to be perfect — it was sort of a works-in-progress recital, to give the dancers a chance to try their routines in public. But Andy's routine had looked completely polished and ready for the professional stage.

It was a modern dance, full of athletic movements and amazing leaps, done to music with a heavy drum beat, which Cary enjoyed. Andy wore a simple red leotard, and she seemed like a flash of fire as the spotlight followed her around the stage.

But even though Andy had brought down the house, even though she'd been just about perfect, Jane could tell the real fire was missing. There was a cold glint in her eyes and a hard set to her jaw, and when she bowed at the end, her smile, which usually warmed everybody in the whole theater, didn't even reach the first row.

So, Jane thought, it was more important than ever to find the mysterious note-writer. Of course, he might not be able to do anything about Andy, either. His notes hadn't exactly thrilled her to pieces. But it might be different in person. And since nobody else was having any luck, why shouldn't he take a chance?

Throwing back the covers, Jane got out of bed and quietly searched the top of her desk until she found a small notebook. She'd decided to make a list of all the places Andy went to regularly. Then, starting the next day, she'd visit each one and see if she could find the boy who was trying to reach Andy's heart.

She was still looking for a pen or a pencil when there was a soft knock at the door. Jane tiptoed across the room, opened the door, and found Maggie standing there holding a small bunch of daisies in her hand.

"Hi," Maggie whispered. "I know we're under strict orders not to touch that care package, but I was afraid Andy might ignore these, too, and I didn't want to see them wilt."

"These are for Andy?" Jane whispered back, taking the flowers.

Maggie nodded. "I found them downstairs when I went for breakfast. And this came with them," she added, holding out a folded note in her other hand.

The two girls grinned at each other. "It's getting better and better, isn't it?" Maggie said.

Jane laughed softly. "It's getting great," she agreed. "And keep your fingers crossed. I have a feeling this is just the beginning."

When Maggie left, Jane put the note and the flowers on Andy's spotless desktop. She was extremely curious about the note, but she knew she couldn't read it first. Her stomach was growling furiously anyway, so she decided to escape from the temptation of peeking at the note by going down to eat.

She stepped into a pair of soft, blue corduroy slacks and was trying to find her favorite hand-knit sweater when the phone rang.

Amazingly, Andy didn't budge.

Jane reached the phone before it rang a second time and picked it up. "Hello?" she said softly.

"Jane?" Toby sounded surprised. "I figured you'd still be sound asleep."

"Toby!" Jane stopped whispering and almost shouted her name. "No, I'm awake. How are you?"

"Fine. Got a pencil?" Toby went on quickly.

"Umm, somewhere, just a second." Jane put the phone down and started frantically pushing things around on her desk.

"Here," Andy said. She was sitting up, wide-eyed and alert, holding out a pen.

"Thanks," Jane took the pen and picked up the phone again. "Toby? Found one."

"Okay, I'm coming back today," Toby said. "Here's the schedule." She gave Jane all of the details, including when her train would come into Greenleaf. "You don't need to call Neal to get me in Boston," she went on. "There's a bus that goes from the airport to the train station and I'll have plenty of time to make it."

"Okay." Jane finished writing everything down and read it back. "Did I get it all?" she asked.

"Yep. So, I'll see you guys late this afternoon," Toby said.

"Wait!" Jane cried. "Toby what's going on? How's your father?"

"Oh." There was a pause. "Well, he's not sick, so you can breathe easy. About that, anyway."

"But — "

"I've got to go now," Toby broke in. "Thanks for coming to meet me. Talk to you then."

Jane hung up and turned to Andy. "Her father's not sick," she said.

"Great!" Andy swung her legs over the side of the bed. "I bet she's really happy."

"I guess," Jane said doubtfully. "She said we could breathe easy. Then she said, 'about that, anyway.' I wonder what she's not breathing easy about."

"We'll find out," Andy said, standing up and touching her toes. As she straightened, she spotted the flowers on her desk. "What's this?"

Jane smiled. "Maggie found them downstairs earlier and brought them up. There's a note, too," she added innocently.

Andy picked up the note, read it, and then tossed it into her wastebasket.

"One of your fans?" Jane asked, trying not to sound too interested.

Andy nodded, obviously not interested at all. "The poet." She yawned and then caught sight of her clock. "Oh, my gosh! I didn't know it was so late. I should have been out of here an hour ago!"

"What for? It's Sunday, and besides, you danced hard last night," Jane said. "You deserve a little extra time in bed."

"I might deserve it, but I can't afford it." Andy hurriedly pulled on her robe and grabbed a towel. "I lost some notes on that

English paper I'm doing, and if I can't find them, I've got to start all over again! Plus I've got a test in Spanish tomorrow, and I haven't put in nearly enough time studying for it."

"What about Toby?" Jane asked as Andy reached the door. "She's coming in at five this afternoon and she expects us to meet her."

Andy stopped. "You mean you can't do it?" she asked.

Jane was tempted to say yes, that's what she meant. After all, Andy wasn't the only one who had things to do. But it wasn't true — she did have time. Besides, she didn't want to get into another argument.

"I can do it," Jane said. "It's just that I thought you'd want to be there, too. And I'm sure Toby would like to see us both."

"You're right." Andy sighed and then shook her head. "But I just can't," she said. "I'll see her tonight, though. Tell her hi for me, will you?"

"Sure." But Jane didn't smile as she said it, and when Andy left, Jane couldn't help feeling disappointed. Being busy was one thing, but being so busy that you couldn't stop for one of your best friends was something else.

She was about to go out to call Cary, to see if he could borrow the lemon again, but as she reached the door she saw the flowers on Andy's desk. Maggie was right — they shouldn't be allowed to wilt. Deciding to get some water for them before she went to eat, she picked them up and then remembered the note.

Eagerly, Jane fished it out of the wastebasket and opened it.

> Dear Andy,
>   I was there last night,
>   As I promised I'd be,
>   And just as I expected,
>   You danced magnificently.
>   P.S. Not a bad rhyme, huh?

Jane laughed out loud. Well, at least the mystery-writer had a sense of humor. Which would help a lot, since Andy seemed to have lost hers. She read the note again, then took the other two out of her purse and read them all.

Who could it be? she wondered. And how would he feel if he knew that Andy tossed his notes away like she did? Would he lose confidence and give up?

Well, when she found him, *if* she found him, Jane just wouldn't tell him, that was all. Because if this boy was really interested in Andy, then he needed all the self-confidence he could get.

CHAPTER EIGHT

Toby's train arrived just as Cary pulled the borrowed car into the station parking lot.

"I don't know which one's chugging worse, the car or the train," Jane joked as they hopped out and ran toward the platform.

"It's a toss-up," Cary agreed. "Just be grateful the heater worked. If you'd walked here, you would have risked frostbite."

Cary was right — it was the coldest day they'd had all winter, and Toby's first comment as she got off the train was, "I thought it was cold back home, but compared to this, we were having a heatwave."

Jane and Cary gave her a quick hug, and then the three of them hustled back to the car. Since Cary had to work at the Greaf, he'd arranged to return the car there, and when Jane suggested that she and Toby eat at the diner, considering what the school served for dinner on Sundays, Toby said "Fine with me." Except for that, she didn't say anything, and Jane knew that everything was far from fine.

When they got to the diner, Jane waited until they'd ordered and Cary was busy with other customers. Then she turned to Toby. "All right," she said, in a no-nonsense voice, "what's going on?"

Toby almost grinned. "Well, don't be shy," she said wryly. "Just come right out and ask me."

Jane had to laugh. She wasn't always so direct; in fact, she'd been taught that it was the height of bad taste to ask about someone's private life. But this was different. "It's hard enough communicating with Andy these days," Jane said. "If you start being like that, I'll go crazy. So tell me what happened in Texas."

Toby took a sip of her milk. "Dad's just fine, like I said."

"And?"

"And . . ." Toby took a deep breath, ". . . and he's in love and he's getting married," she said quickly.

Jane's mouth almost dropped open, but she caught herself in time. "Married? That's . . ." she started to say wonderful, but changed her mind at the look on Toby's face. ". . . um, interesting and surprising," she finished.

Toby nodded.

"What's her name?" Jane asked.

"Emma," Toby said. "Emma Barkin."

Jane waited. Cary set down their plates and rushed off to another table. Jane buttered a roll. "Well?" she finally asked, determined not to let Toby clam up, "What's this Emma Barkin like? Is she nice?"

Toby thought back to yesterday morning, when she'd finally ridden back to the ranch to meet her father's ladyfriend, as he called her. Emma Barkin had just arrived, and she and Mr. Houston had watched, standing together and holding hands, as Toby rode up.

What was Emma Barkin like? Toby thought. Well, she was tall and slender. Her short, curly hair was brown with a little gray in it, and her eyes were blue. She had a firm handshake and an easy smile. She admitted right off that she didn't know much about ranches or horses or cattle, since she'd been living and working as an accountant in Dallas. But she asked so many questions — not dumb ones, either—that Toby knew she was genuinely interested in learning. So Toby couldn't hold that against her.

In fact, during the entire day she'd spent at the ranch, Toby couldn't find much of anything to hold against Emma Barkin. She and Toby's father might have fallen in love only a few months ago, but they acted like they'd been good friends for a long time.

With Emma Barkin, Toby's father laughed and joked and actually talked in paragraphs once in a while. He was happy, Toby could tell.

Toby picked up her toasted cheese sandwich and took a bite. Swallowing, she said, "Yep. She seems real nice."

"Finally!" Jane sighed. "I was beginning to think you'd gone into a trance. Good," she went on, "I'm glad she's nice. Is your father happy?"

"Yep."

"Well?" Jane decided to get right to the point again. "What's the matter?"

Toby ate some more of her sandwich, thinking about it. Finally she said, "I guess I just figured nothing would change. That it would always be my father and me and the ranch. I didn't count on somebody else sharing it."

Jane wasn't sure what to say. She knew this was a big change in Toby's life, but she thought it could be a good one. And Toby was already treating it like it was bad. She drank some tea and then asked, "Do you want my opinion?"

Toby smiled. "Aren't I going to get it anyway?"

"Yes," Jane laughed. "All right, here's what I think. I think you ought to give Emma Barkin and your father a chance, at least. You said you always thought it would be just you and him and the ranch. I suppose it could be, but it probably won't."

"Why not?"

"Well, just think about it!" Jane urged. "You're not finished with high school yet. After this, you'll probably go to college. Then you'll get a job. And who knows where that job will be?" She took another sip of tea and smiled. "And guess what? *You* might even fall in love sometime in there and decide to get married yourself."

Toby smiled too. "I usually don't think that far ahead."

"I don't, either," Jane admitted. "But I'm almost positive some of those things will happen. And that you won't be spending the entire rest of your life on the ranch with your father. I'm positive he doesn't expect you to, either."

"You're right," Toby said, picking up the other half of her sandwich. "I guess I was being downright selfish, when you think about it. I want Dad to be happy, and he sure seems happy with Emma Barkin." She ate hungrily for a minute, then stopped, blushing as she thought about the way she'd acted yesterday.

Not only had she been selfish, she'd been almost rude. There was her father, obviously in love, but also a little nervous and worried about how Toby was feeling. There was Emma, as pleasant as could be. She didn't act nervous, but Toby realized she must have been, hoping she'd make a good impression, hoping Toby would like her.

And there *I* was, Toby thought, mumbling one-word answers and walking around with my chin practically dragging the ground. She almost cringed when she thought about this morning, when her father had driven her back to the airport. He hadn't said a word, but when he hugged her good-bye, Toby could see in his eyes that he was disappointed in the way she'd acted.

Toby picked up her milk and finished it in one swallow. "We're not waiting for Cary to drive us back to the dorm in that overheated tin can, are we?" she asked.

Jane laughed. "No, he had to return it."

"Good," Toby said, wiping her mouth and getting up. "We can get there faster on foot, anyway."

"What's the rush?" Jane asked, getting up, too, and following Toby to the cashier's desk.

"I've got to make a phone call and set something straight," Toby said. "Then everything will be right as rain."

"I won't pretend to understand that," Jane remarked.

Toby grinned. "Translation: I've got to call my father and tell him I think Emma's a terrific woman and I'm as tickled pink as he is," she explained.

"Now *that* makes sense," Jane said. "And

when you're finished, I've got something else for you to do."

"What?"

Jane smiled as they headed out into the frosty air. "You're going to help me solve a mystery," she said.

While Jane and Cary had been driving as fast as the law and the car allowed to meet Toby's train, Andy found herself trudging over piles of snow and slipping on icy sidewalks, hurrying to get to the Greenleaf Library before it closed. She'd searched her room, her desk, the study room in Baker House and the rehearsal room in the theater building, but she still hadn't found the notes for her research paper.

Then she'd gone to the Canby Hall library, hoping that Gigi Norton had pulled off a miracle and finished her paper. But the first person Andy spotted when she walked in was the Worst Person in the World herself, taking up an entire table, poring over the very books Andy needed.

For one desperate moment, Andy considered asking Gigi if she could borrow them, just for a couple of hours. But then Gigi had glanced up and smirked.

The smirk did it. Andy spun around, pulled up the collar of her jacket, and headed for the Greenleaf Library.

As she walked, she saw a small rusty car

chugging down the street ahead of her, and she realized it was the lemon she'd teased Cary about. Without thinking, she raised her hand and waved, but the car drove on, made a slow turn at the corner, and sputtered out of sight.

Andy wasn't sure why she'd waved. She really couldn't take the time to go to the station. Not now, especially. But she knew if Cary or Jane had seen her and stopped the car, she would have hopped in anyway. True, Toby's father was well, and Toby didn't really need three people to meet her at the train station. Jane had been right, though — Toby would have been glad to see her, and Andy had been feeling guilty about not going all afternoon. Now, walking along the icy path, she felt not only guilty, she felt lonely. It would have been fun to meet Toby and hear about Texas, and maybe stop off at the Greaf for dinner.

Then Andy gave herself a mental shake. Having fun didn't get anything done. And she had plenty to do, thanks to Gigi Norton. When she got back to the dorm, she could talk to Toby and find out what was happening. Toby would understand why she hadn't come to the station.

The Greenleaf Library closed early on Sunday evenings, and when Andy walked in, she discovered that she had exactly fifteen minutes to find the book. Or her notes. When she'd returned the book, she'd had the notebook with her — maybe she'd dropped it in there.

Since it was so near closing time, there was a crowd at the desk, and Andy had to spend six of her precious minutes waiting in line. Finally, it was her turn. "Do you have a lost and found box?" she asked the woman.

"Yes, we do." The woman motioned Andy to the end of the counter, then pulled a large cardboard box from underneath. "I'm supposed to ask what you're looking for, but I'll have a riot on my hands if I take the time," she said. "I can trust you not to take anything unless it's yours, can't I?"

Andy nodded in what she hoped was a trustworthy way. Then she dug into the box. Who'd want to steal any of this stuff anyway, she thought, as she pushed aside mittens, scarves, a few well-chewed pencils, at least five empty eyeglass cases and one decrepit baby rattle. It didn't take long to discover that her notebook wasn't there. Eight minutes gone.

Thanking the woman, Andy sped past the counter and headed for the stacks, crossing her fingers as she got to the spot where the book would be shelved if it was there. Which it wasn't.

Now what? she wondered, her mind racing. The book would be back in three days and she didn't want to take any chances on missing it again. She'd reserve it, that's what she'd do. A buzzer sounded, making her jump. Five minutes until the library closed. If she wanted to reserve the book, she'd better hurry.

Almost running, Andy dashed to the end of the row, turned the corner and immediately collided with the book cart, which was being pushed in her direction at an extremely unsafe speed.

"Ow!" Andy cried, bending down and rubbing her shin.

"Hey, watch it!" somebody else cried at the same time.

Andy was almost hopping in pain; she came down on one foot and landed on a pile of books that had slipped off the cart during the collision. Covered in shiny protective jackets, they were slippery, and Andy lost her balance and fell to the floor. As she was struggling to get up, another book slid from the cart and bounced off her head.

"It's an interesting theory, but it'll never work," someone said, and Andy looked up to see the same boy she'd talked to a few days before.

"What won't work?" she asked, getting to her feet.

He pointed to her head. "Trying to learn by hitting yourself over the head with books," he said seriously. "Skulls are very hard. The facts just bounce right off."

Andy frowned at him.

"I wasn't trying to learn anything, at least not from this book," she said, picking it up and putting it on the cart. "I was trying to find something. And if you hadn't been going over the speed limit, I might have had a chance."

"Pardon me," he said. "I just never expected to find somebody training for the Boston Marathon in the library. Most people do their running outdoors."

Andy breathed deeply and started counting to ten. He interrupted her before she got to three. "What were you trying to find?"

"A book," she said.

"You've come to the right place," he remarked. "Title?"

Andy rattled it off, fuming inside.

"I remember now," he said. "It's — "

"I know," Andy broke in. "It's a three-day book. I was on my way to reserve it when you hit me."

He raised his eyebrows. "I won't comment on that."

"Fine." Andy took a step and stumbled over the pile of books on the floor. "I only have a minute to get to the desk and reserve it," she said, catching her balance before she fell again. "The least you could do is. . . ."

"Correction," he said, pointing to the clock over the main door. "You have no minutes to get to the desk. The library's closed." He smiled for the first time. "The least I can do is show you the way out."

Andy didn't answer. Taking another deep breath, she stepped around the spilled books and strode toward the door. She didn't look back, but she felt his eyes on her all the way.

CHAPTER NINE

This time, Toby wasn't surprised that she was able to reach her father. Whenever she went back to school, she always let him know she'd arrived safely. So she knew he'd be at the ranch waiting for her call.

"Glad to hear it," he said when she told him. He did sound glad, but Toby thought she heard something else in his voice. Probably feels like asking me where my manners went, she thought.

"I'm back and I'm fine," she said again. "But that's not the only reason I called, Dad."

"No?"

"No. I wanted to say I'm sorry. I was pretty rude to Miss . . . Mrs . . . um . . ." Toby wasn't sure what to call her.

Her father chuckled. "Why don't you just settle for Emma?"

"Good. Anyway," Toby went on, "I was rude, and I'm sorry. If Emma was there,

I'd apologize to her, too, so will you do it for me when you see her again?"

"Be happy to."

"When *will* you see her again?" Toby asked.

"In about half an hour," he said. "I'm takin' her into Rio Verde for supper."

"Rio Verde! Dad, there's no place to eat there," Toby said.

"There's Boyce's Café," he reminded her, mentioning the only place to get food in town, not counting the candy machine at the gas station.

"Like I said," Toby repeated, "there's no place to eat there." She shook her head. Even though it was surrounded by some of the best ranchland in Texas, Boyce's couldn't even cook a decent steak. "Emma deserves better than that."

"I agree, but we can't drive four hours to — " Mr. Houston broke off. "What was that, Toby?"

"I said Emma deserves better than that." Toby smiled into the phone. "What I'm trying to say is I'm happy for you. For both of you. I think it's going to be great, Dad."

Mr. Houston cleared his throat, a sure sign that he was too pleased to speak.

"There's plenty of chili in the freezer. You can defrost it in the oven. And you better do it," Toby warned, "because if you plan on getting married, and you take

Emma to Rio Verde for supper, you just might never see her again."

When Toby hung up, she felt better than she had in a week. Now she was ready to get back to the rest of her life.

"Well?" Jane asked when Toby came into 407. "Is everything right as rain?"

Toby nodded happily.

"That's great. How did your father react?"

"He didn't say much."

Jane laughed. "That's a good sign."

"Yep," Toby agreed, pulling off her boots and sitting cross-legged on her bed. "Now, what's this mystery I'm supposed to help you solve?"

"Here." Jane took the three notes from her purse, put them in order and handed them to Toby. "Read these first. Then I'll explain."

Toby read them carefully, her smile getting wider with each one. "Well, well," she said when she'd finished. "Looks like somebody's interested in being Andy's beau."

"Somebody's *very* interested," Jane said, pointing to the flowers. "He sent her those with the last note. The big problem is that Andy's not interested in having a 'beau.' "

"No, I guess she wouldn't be," Toby agreed.

"But she might be if she met him," Jane pointed out.

"Oh, I get it," Toby said. "You want to find him and sort of help things along."

Jane bit into a peanut butter cracker and nodded. "Andy's made up her mind not to take any more chances after Ramad," she said. Then she told Toby what Andy had said about never letting something like that happen again. "That's why she's acting the way she is — so she'll be too busy to let it happen." She took the notes from Toby and held them up as if they were pieces of evidence in a courtroom. "I'm hoping whoever wrote these can make it happen. But first we have to find him."

Toby couldn't help laughing. "I never thought I'd see proper Jane Barrett sticking her nose into someone else's business," she said.

"I don't plan to make a habit of it," Jane said with a smile. "But I think this is important. Somebody's got to do something."

"Maybe." Toby looked a little doubtful. "But what if Andy doesn't like the whole idea? I mean, she could get real mad if she caught us interfering like that."

"She could," Jane agreed, "*if* she caught us."

"This is a secret mission, huh?" Toby grinned and then shook her head. "I'm still not sure it's the right thing to do. Seems like Andy has a right to decide for herself whether she wants to see this guy, or any guy."

Jane started to argue, but just then, Andy burst into the room. For a moment both her roommates wondered if she'd been listening at the door, because Andy was obviously very angry about something.

"I'm so mad I could spit!" she announced, dropping her duffel bag on the bed and flopping down beside it. "Talk about creeps!"

"Who's a creep?" Jane asked guiltily.

"Some guy at the Greenleaf Library," Andy said, staring at the ceiling.

Jane breathed a sigh of relief. At least Andy hadn't overheard their conversation. "What did he do?"

Andy held up her hand and started ticking off the boy's offenses on her finger. "First of all, he was pushing that cart around like he was in the Indy 500. Then he didn't even bother to apologize when he crashed it into me. Next he kept insulting me until it was too late for me to reserve the book I need. And last" — she stopped long enough to take a breath — "he had the nerve to smile when he practically threw me out!"

"You've got one finger left," Toby observed. "Didn't the creep do anything else?"

"Toby!" Andy shot up into a sitting position. "I didn't even see you when I came in!"

"Well, here I am," Toby smiled.

"How's your father?" Andy asked. "Jane said he was healthy, but that something else was bothering you. Is he really okay?"

"He's more than okay," Toby said. "He's in love and he's going to get married." She went on to tell Andy all about Emma Barkin and the big romance, but halfway through, she got the feeling that Andy had stopped listening. Maybe Andy didn't understand what a big deal this was in her life and her father's life, she thought. After all, Mrs. Cord was still alive; Andy and her father didn't have any idea what it was like to be on their own together for years, without anyone else.

"Listen to me," she laughed, deciding not to say anymore about it. "I sound like a real dope, talking about romance like this."

"No, that's okay," Andy said. "I think it's a great thing, for your father." She gave Toby one of her big smiles, the kind that Jane had decided looked like a marionette's smile. Then she stood up and started to undress.

Toby glanced at Jane, who raised her eyebrows. Now Toby got it. It wasn't that Andy didn't understand about romance, it was just that she couldn't bear to hear about it.

"Anyway," Andy was saying, "thanks to that creep in the library, I couldn't even reserve that book, and I'm going to have to go back there in three days and try to grab it before somebody else does." She pulled on a long, multi-colored kimono and stepped into a pair of pink slippers. "Of course," she went on, "part of it's Gigi Norton's fault, too."

"What did that person do?" Jane asked.

"She beat me to every book the Canby Hall library has on Eugene O'Neill," Andy said. "I get the feeling she's going to keep renewing them until the day the paper's due."

Jane nodded, as if nothing Gigi did would ever surprise her. "I take it you didn't find your notebook," she said. She felt like mentioning that Andy's predicament was partly Andy's fault, too, since she lost the notebook. But she decided she'd better not; Andy might think she was trying to rub it in.

"You're right," Andy said, "I didn't find that notebook, and I spent so much time looking for it that I never got around to studying for my Spanish test." She picked up her Spanish book and started for the door. "So, I thought I'd go downstairs and hole up in one of the study rooms for the next three hours, at least. If you're still up when I get back," she added, going into the hall, "let's talk about the Winter Festival. It's coming up, you know, so we don't have much time to make posters and get everything organized."

Andy turned to walk away and nearly tripped over something just outside the door. "I almost forgot," she said. She stepped back into the room carrying a large box wrapped in brown paper, which she slid under her bed. "There," she said, giving them another big smile. "See you later."

When she'd gone, Jane and Toby stared at each other for a moment. Finally, Jane got out of her chair, went over to Andy's bed and looked underneath.

"Is it what I think it is?" Toby sounded amazed.

"Exactly," Jane said indignantly.

"The care package?"

"The one and only."

Toby whistled. "I was sort of hoping she would have opened it by the time I got back."

"No such luck," Jane said, straightening up. "I can't believe she brought it in right under our very noses and then stuck it under the bed without saying a word about it."

"Speaking of noses," Toby said, "does it smell?"

"Not yet." Jane got her package of peanut butter crackers, offered one to Toby and took one for herself. "I guess we'll have to survive on these until Andy comes to her senses," she said, frowning at the cracker before she bit into it. "Now you see what I mean, don't you — that we have to do something?"

Toby nodded thoughtfully. "You know, when I was talking about Dad, I expected her to be happy for him. And I guess she was, but mostly she was thinking about Ramad and feeling sorry for herself." She reached for another cracker. "It kind of hurt my feelings, and Andy's not like that."

"It *was* a selfish reaction," Jane agreed. "But it's good, in a way."

"It was?" Toby looked skeptical. "What's good about it?"

"It means her plan's not working," Jane said. "If she can feel sorry for herself, then we know she's not as hard-hearted as she's trying to be. Which means she can feel good and happy again, too. But she needs something — or someone — to feel happy about."

Toby picked up the three notes. "And that brings us back to this guy," she said with a grin.

"It's worth a try isn't it?" Jane asked. "We've been leaving her alone all this time, and things aren't getting any better. Besides," she added, her blue eyes sparkling, "it's been awfully dull around here lately. Tracking down a mysterious admirer could be a lot of fun."

"Okay," Toby laughed. "I always did like a good mystery, so count me in. Where do we start?"

Jane dug out the notebook where she'd started to list the places Andy went, and explained the theory she and Cary had come up with — that the secret admirer was someone who saw Andy almost regularly.

"That makes sense," Toby agreed. "I just have one question — what are we going to do when we find him?"

"First, we have to make sure he's really interested in Andy," Jane said, "that he's not just playing a game. I don't think he is, though. Sending flowers in the middle of winter is kind of an expensive game."

Toby nodded.

"And we have to approve of him, naturally," Jane added.

"Approve?" Toby hooted. "You make it sound like he's got to pass some kind of test."

"He does," Jane said seriously. "He has to be a nice person, not a creep."

"Okay, I can't argue with that," Toby said. "So, let's say we find him. He's not playing games and he's not a creep. What do we do then? Lock him and Andy in a room together? Tell Andy we found a nice person we want her to meet?" She shook her head. "Somehow, I don't think she'll be exactly thrilled."

Jane thought a minute, and then shook her head. "We'll figure out what to do when we find him," she decided. "First, let's find him." She pointed to Andy's bed, where the care package had been shoved. "And let's do it fast. I'm getting sick and tired of peanut butter crackers!"

CHAPTER TEN

By Monday morning, Jane and Toby were ready with their plan of action. Jane would station herself at the Greaf as often as possible (which was not really a sacrifice, since the food was better than the dining hall's and Cary was there), and see if she could find someone who might be the mysterious admirer.

Toby's assignment was the theater building, where she'd try to do the same thing. It was a busy place — boys from Oakley Prep used it, too — and she and Jane had high hopes for it. After all, writing anonymous notes was a very theatrical thing to do; the secret admirer just might be an actor who'd found a real-life role to play.

Since Canby Hall was a girls' school, the classrooms, dining hall, and study halls were out. But the library was open to the public, so Toby and Jane planned to check it out, too.

"If we don't find him in any of those places," Jane said, "then we'll try some of the stores, and maybe the movies. He could be working taking tickets there or working at the popcorn stand."

"Yeah, but Andy hasn't been going to any movies lately," Toby pointed out.

"I know," Jane agreed. "The movies and the stores are on my fall-back list."

"Listen to the new Jane Barrett," Toby teased. "You're getting to be as organized as Andy with your plans and lists."

"Something as important as this takes planning and organization." Jane surveyed the mess on her side of the room and laughed. "I'm sloppy, but not with things that really count."

The two of them were getting ready for breakfast and classes. Andy, as usual, was already up and gone. When she'd come upstairs from studying the night before, Jane and Toby were already asleep. When they woke, the first thing they saw was a large piece of paper taped to the inside of the door. WINTER FESTIVAL!!! was printed across it in purple magic marker, and the words were underlined at least fifteen times.

Looking at it now, Toby said, "Do you get the feeling she's trying to tell us something?"

Jane giggled. "The feeling I really get is that she wished she'd never come up with the idea for a winter festival. I mean, P.A.'s on her back about it all the time," she explained, "plus Andy's in charge of the whole thing and it's turning out to be a lot of work."

"Seems like all we need is snow and ice." Toby said. "And we've sure got plenty of that."

"That's just the beginning," Jane told her. "There has to be a refreshment stand — Penny's in charge of that. Dee's supposed to be organizing the teams, and Maggie's trying to think up silly prizes to hand out."

"What about us?" Toby asked. "Don't tell me we got off scot-free."

"Hardly. We've been assigned to make posters and put them up all over the place so everybody will know what's happening." Jane giggled again and pointed to Andy's sign on the door. "I'm pretty sure that was a hint — we're not doing our job fast enough."

"We're not doing it at all," Toby pointed out dryly.

They'd just started to discuss the posters they had to make when there was a sudden, piercing shriek out in the hall.

Jane dropped her shoes, ran to the door and pulled it open. Up and down the hall-way, girls had stuck their heads out of their rooms to see what had happened.

"What is it?" Toby asked anxiously, coming up behind Jane and poking her head out, too.

"I don't know. I can't see anything."

"There's Andy," Toby said. "Andy!" she called, "what was that noise?"

From the far end of the hall, Andy looked up, opened her mouth and shrieked again, wildly waving a manila envelope over her head.

"Well, we know what the noise was," Toby remarked as Andy raced toward 407. "Now all we have to do is find out what caused it."

Breathless and smiling, Andy ran into the room, tossed the envelope into the air and whooped with delight. "Just look!" she shouted, catching the envelope in one hand. Opening it, she pulled out a spiral notebook and kissed it. "I'm saved!"

"Your research notes?" Jane asked.

"Yes, can you believe it?" Andy cried. "It was on the desk downstairs when I came back from beakfast!"

Toby and Jane looked at each other. "The mail doesn't come this early," Toby said. "Somebody must have delivered it in person."

"Who cares how it got here?" Andy laughed. "It's here, that's the important thing. Now I don't have to wait around for those books, or for Gigi Norton to have a complete personality change."

Still laughing happily, Andy gathered up the rest of the papers and books she needed for morning classes and dashed back out the door.

"Hmm," Jane said when she'd gone. "The mystery goes on."

"And on," Toby said, pointing to a folded piece of paper lying on the floor. "I'm willing to bet my bottom dollar that note fell out of the same envelope Andy was just carrying on about."

"Save your dollar," Jane told her, picking up the note. "I just know this is a clue, and we can't afford to overlook it."

Unfolding the paper, she read aloud, " 'Dear Andy, I was glancing around, and look what I found. When you get it you'll smile, I hope for a while.' "

Toby laughed. "That's not any better than the other ones."

"True," Jane agreed. "His poetry is definitely not improving." She put the note back on the floor for Andy to find, even though she knew it would eventually wind up in the trash. "But at least he hasn't given up. And neither will we."

Jane hoped she'd make it to the Greaf for lunch, but she *did* have classes, after all. Even though the mystery seemed much more exciting than her school work right now, she could hardly flunk out while she tried to solve it. So it was late afternoon before she got to the diner.

Without even asking, Cary brought her a large Coke and put in an order for a cheeseburger and fries.

"How'd you guess?" she asked.

"Easy. You have the look of someone who ate lunch in the dining hall," Cary told her. "Sort of a greenish tinge to your face and a glazed look in your eyes."

"You're kidding, I hope."

"Of course I'm kidding," he said seriously. "Except for the green color, you look great."

"I should have known better than to ask," Jane laughed.

"True," Cary agreed. He went off to take some more orders, then came back with Jane's food. "So. What's going on?"

"Toby and I are officially trying to find Andy's mystery man," Jane announced. "She got another note this morning and — "

"I knew it!" Cary said, slapping his forehead. "I kept telling myself not to forget, but I knew I'd forget and I did!"

Jane was busy chewing and could only raise her eyebrows to ask what he was talking about.

"The mystery man," Cary said. "I think I may have found him."

Jane swallowed so quickly she almost choked. "How? Where?"

"Wait." Cary sped off to get some more orders, delivered them to the booths and then dashed back. "I just noticed it yesterday," he said. "Andy's been coming in here a lot lately, getting juice and stuff to go. Well, yesterday, there was this guy in here, too. Watching her."

"Andy's awfully pretty," Jane reminded him. "I'm sure plenty of guys enjoy watching her."

"Yes, but I'm not finished," Cary said. "I realized yesterday that this guy has been in here before. And some of those times, Andy was in here, too!" he said triumphantly.

"This is great!" Jane said excitedly. "When does he usually come in?"

"It's hard to tell, since I'm not here all the time. But I think . . . wait!" he said again. Then he leaned across the counter and lowered his voice. "Yes," he whispered. "You're in luck. He just walked in the door."

Jane had to fight the urge to turn around and stare, but she managed to conquer it. "What's he doing?" she whispered back.

"Looking for a place to sit." Cary's eyes were sparkling — he was obviously enjoying this. "Ah-ha! He found one — a booth over by the window."

"Is it one of your tables?"

"Unfortunately not." Cary started wiping the counter, which turned a corner at one end. He casually worked his way down and around until he was closer to the stranger, then came back.

"What's he doing?" Jane asked.

"Giving his order," Cary reported. "He's staring out the window now. Quick! Look over your left shoulder."

Trying not to appear too obvious, Jane spun around on her chair. Most of what she saw from her angle was the back of a man's head, but she did notice that he was wearing a thick wool sweater in a beautiful shade of blue.

"He's got good taste in clothes, at least," she said, turning back around. "Andy would love that sweater."

"Don't get carried away yet," Cary laughed. "First you have to find out if he's the right one."

"I know, that's the hard part." Jane smiled. "I don't suppose you'd like to do it, would you? After all, you're good at striking up conversations with people you've never met."

"I may be good, but I'm also late," Cary said. "I have to rehearse with Ambulance in about five minutes, and even though I'm fleet of foot, I'll never make it."

"I thought you were working here."

"I was, until two minutes ago." Cary untied the white apron from around his waist, leaned across the counter and kissed Jane on the cheek. "My shift is over," he told her, and with a grin, he tilted his head in the direction of the window booth. "Yours is just beginning."

After Cary left, Jane risked another look

toward the window. He had a glass of soda now, plus a fork and a knife. Good, she thought, he ordered food. That means he won't be leaving for a while. Now I can . . . what?

Jane hadn't really thought this part out very carefully. Would he think she was crazy if she just walked over, showed him the notes, and asked if he wrote them? Yes, he probably would. Or he might be too embarrassed to admit it. Or he might say he did, just for a joke. No, she had to be very subtle and very clever about this, she decided.

While Jane was trying to think of a subtle approach, a group of five people came up to the counter. Four of them sat down on Jane's right. All the stools to the left were taken, except for one, and it was around the corner, at the very end.

Jane graciously offered her seat to the fifth person in the group, picked up her plate and glass and took it to the end of the counter. A perfect opportunity, she thought, smiling to herself as she sat down.

Now for the really hard part. She nibbled on a french fry, trying to think of what to do next, started to reach for the salt, and then stopped. Glancing left and right, she made sure that no one was paying attention, then stuck out her finger and poked at the saltshaker until it tipped over and fell behind the counter.

The Greaf wasn't known for its hushed atmosphere, so no one heard the saltshaker land. Cary's replacement had just gone through the swinging doors into the kitchen, so he wouldn't see it for a while. The nearest other saltshaker was ten stools away, except, of course, for the one where the guy was sitting.

Jane spun around on her stool, pretended to be looking for something, caught his eye, and said, "May I borrow your salt, please? Mine seems to be missing."

He stopped drinking his soda and handed her the salt. He looked a little puzzled, but all he said was "Sure."

"Thank you very much."

"Sure."

Jane turned back to her fries. He was nice-looking, she decided, with a close-cut Afro and handsome, long-fingered hands. And his voice was soft, what she'd heard of it. But was he the one? Two "sures" weren't enough to go on.

With another poke of Jane's finger, the pepper went off the counter. "Excuse me," she said, turning around again, "do you mind if I borrow your pepper, too?"

His food had arrived, and he was busy putting ketchup on his burger, but he stopped long enough to hand her the pepper. This time, he didn't say a word.

This is not getting you anywhere, Jane told herself as she peppered the remaining two bites of her cheeseburger. There had to be some way to get the information she wanted without being obvious about it.

Glancing around the diner again, she happened to notice a headline in the newspaper that one of the customers was reading, and it gave her the approach she'd been looking for. She dug into her purse and pulled out a small notepad and pencil, then turned back to the window booth.

"I'm sorry to bother you," she said, "but I've been assigned to do a survey for my social studies class, and I wonder if you'd mind answering a few questions."

Swallowing quickly, the boy checked his watch, and then nodded. "All right," he said. "If it won't take long."

"No, I'll be very fast," Jane promised, smiling brightly. She flipped open the pad and got her pencil ready. "First question — are you a student?"

He nodded again. "Just transferred to Oakley Prep about six weeks ago."

That fits, Jane thought, scribbling something down. It gives him just enough time to have settled in and discover Andy. "What's your favorite subject?"

"English."

Even better, she thought. Somebody who likes English probably tries to write poetry. "And" — she pretended to check her next question — "do you have any hobbies?" The answer didn't matter, but she thought she ought to throw in some survey-type questions.

"I like to write programs on my computer," he said. "And bicycle racing."

"Mmm." Jane made some more illegible marks on her pad, and then decided to get to the point. Smiling brightly again, she said, "this may seem a little personal, but it's part of the assignment — how often do you date?" This survey was a great idea, she thought. She could ask just about anything without seeming to pry.

"Date?" he asked with a laugh. "It's pretty hard to get a date at Oakley Prep."

"Of course," Jane said smoothly. "But what about Canby Hall?"

"Oh, right, that must be where you go."

Jane nodded, her pencil poised.

"Well," he laughed again, "I've heard about Canby Hall, but that's it."

"That's it? What do you mean?"

"I mean I haven't been anywhere near it since I got to Greenleaf," he explained. "Oakley's tough. I'm really snowed under with homework."

Jane lowered her pencil.

"But," he went on, "even if I weren't so busy, I wouldn't be interested. See, I've got a girlfriend back home. We've been going together since seventh grade, and we dated about three times a week." He paused. "You didn't write that down."

"Oh." Jane drew an X through the rest

of her scribbles. "Well, thank you very much," she said, trying not to sound disappointed.

"You mean that's all?" he asked.

She nodded. "I told you it wouldn't take long. Thanks again."

"Sure." He gave her a confused smile. "Can I ask *you* a question now?"

Jane wasn't in the mood, but she decided he deserved it. "All right," she said. "Go ahead."

"Okay. Here goes." He slid out of the booth, walked around behind the counter, and picked up her salt and pepper shakers. "I was just wondering," he said, "why you shoved these off."

CHAPTER
ELEVEN

"It wasn't funny at all," Jane insisted for at least the tenth time. "It was extremely embarrassing."

"Sorry," Cary said, stifling another laugh. "I just can't help it. Dumping your salt and pepper shakers is a new way to break the ice. I'll have to try it some time."

Jane tried to frown at him, but it was impossible, and she found herself laughing, too. "I hadn't thought of the survey idea yet," she said. "Next time I'll know exactly what to do, and I won't have to spill anything."

It was the day after Jane's encounter with the non-mystery man, and she and Cary were walking together to the stationery store to buy poster paper and magic markers. The Winter Festival was only days away, and as Andy had mentioned every half-hour last night, only about six people even knew about it.

"What exactly is this festival, anyway?" Cary asked.

"Just a way to break up the monotony of winter," Jane said. "Games and contests — sled races, building snowpeople, a snowball fight between the dorms. The Greenleaf High School's having one and Andy thought Canby Hall should, too."

"Sounds like fun," Cary commented, pushing open the door to the stationery store.

"It better be," Jane remarked. "Because getting ready for it sure isn't. Andy's so serious about it, we feel like we're planning a funeral instead of a festival. Of course," she added, "if we find her secret admirer, then everything might change."

Jane walked down an aisle until she found the magic markers and was choosing the colors she needed when Cary, two aisles over, said "Psst!"

"What?"

Cary wiggled his eyebrows up and down and waved her over. "Look," he said softly, when she'd joined him.

Jane looked and saw a boy at the far end of Cary's aisle taking boxes of typing paper from a supply cart and putting them on the shelf. He obviously worked in the store.

Jane had completely forgotten about him, but then, she hadn't been in here in weeks. Andy had, though. She was making so many lists and doing so much extra work that she went through enough notebooks and pencils to keep this place in business by herself. She could have lost her glove in here and the notes for that paper!

Bob, that was his name, Jane remembered now. Maybe Bob had suddenly discovered Andy and was too shy to come right out and say it.

"Well," Cary whispered, "are you ready to take your survey?"

Jane shook her head. "He knows me," she said. "I don't think I could do the survey with someone I know."

"He goes to Oakley," Cary said. "I've seen him around, but we don't really know each other." He wiggled his eyebrows again. "You want me to handle it?"

"Be my guest," Jane told him. "Just don't be too obvious about it."

"Never fear," Cary assured her with a grin. "I can be a master of subtlety when I have to."

Jane went back to the magic markers and listened as Cary casually struck up a conversation with Bob. First they talked about Oakley. Then they commiserated about how hard it was to hold a part-time job and study, too. Then they moved on to girls.

"You're lucky," Bob told Cary. He lowered his voice. Jane, on her knees so she wouldn't appear to be eavesdropping, had to strain to hear. "I mean, I know you've got a girlfriend. I saw her come in with you. Jane, right?"

"Oh, you know her?" Cary asked innocently.

"Sure. Anyway," Bob went on, "I don't. Have a girlfriend, that is."

So far, so good, Jane thought.

"Well," Cary said, "Canby Hall *is* just a stone's throw away from Oakley, you know."

"Tell me about it," Bob laughed. "Oh, I date, but it sure would be nice to find somebody, you know, special."

"Yeah," Cary agreed. "It's great." Jane heard him snap his fingers. "Well, listen," he said, as if she'd just thought of it, "if you know Jane then you must know her roommate!"

A master of subtlety? Jane thought with a wry smile.

"Oh, you mean . . ." Bob paused. "I can't remember her name. Curly red hair, southern accent?"

"Toby," Cary said. "Sure. And their other roommate, too. Andy. Andy Cord."

Jane's feet were asleep but she didn't want to move. This was the crucial part.

"Andy?" Bob whistled and Jane was sure he was about to confide everything to Cary. Then he said, "You know, I used to like her."

Used to? Jane thought.

"Used to?" Cary asked.

"Well, lately . . ." Bob lowered his voice even more, "she's been driving me crazy! She used to be fun, you know? But when she comes in here these days, she's all business. No time to talk or joke. And if I have to get something for her from the stockroom, she taps her foot and watches the clock like somebody's holding a stopwatch on her." He whistled again. "I don't know what her problem is, but I'm looking to have fun, not run a race."

A few minutes later, Jane and Cary were back outside. Jane was extremely annoyed. "How could he say those things about Andy?" she fumed. "I have half a mind to stop buying supplies there."

"It's the only stationery store in town. Besides," Cary reminded her, "you've said the same things about Andy yourself."

That was true, Jane had to admit. Andy *had* changed, and Bob was just being honest about it. "Well," she said, "at least we know he's not the secret admirer."

"Right," Cary laughed. "If he sent her anything, it would probably be a carton of supplies, just to get her off his back." He took Jane's hand as they hurried along the icy sidewalk. "Don't worry about it. You'll find the guy. Or maybe Toby will."

"That's right," Jane said, remembering. "She's at the theater building right now. I hope she's having better luck than I am."

*   *   *

Toby wasn't just in the theater building. She was up high in the theater building, crouched on a catwalk about twenty feet above the auditorium seats.

"This is one of the big spots," Richie was telling her, pointing to a light aimed at the stage. "There's one at the other end, too, and we work them by hand whenever we need to follow anybody around." He swung the light, demonstrating, and the catwalk swayed slightly. Toby clutched its edges and waited for it to stop.

On stage, Andy and some of the other dance students were working on a routine. None of them paid any attention to Toby and Richie. They probably don't know we're up here, Toby thought, wishing she weren't.

She hadn't planned it, of course. But when she'd come here, hoping to find a boy who might be interested in Andy, the first person she'd run into had been Richie. Toby didn't know him, but he was very outgoing and friendly, and it wasn't long before he'd told her almost everything about himself.

He was from Oakley Prep. This was his first year there, and Toby figured he must have transferred, because he looked old enough to be a senior. He loved the theater. He also loved peach ice cream, Chinese food, and cocker spaniels. He didn't know much about dance, but he admired the dancers, because they worked so hard, especially Andy.

Toby's ears had perked up at this. So far, she'd asked him only one question, and by now, she knew more about him than she really wanted to. Except, of course, for the important thing — was he the note writer?

Not that Richie seemed like the kind of guy who would write anonymous notes. Toby thought that if he was interested in somebody, he'd come right out and tell her . . . and tell her . . . and tell her.

"Hey, Richie?" she said, her first words in at least twenty minutes. "I hope you don't mind, but I never was very good when it came to heights. Airplanes are fine, because I'm closed in, but out in the open, the highest I like to get is on top of my horse."

"Oh, you ride?" Richie asked, seeming to ignore everything else she said. "My roommate rides. He's on an equestrian team, as a matter of fact. I rode with him once — boy, that was something! Those jumps are harder than they look.

"Of course," he went on, "growing up in Detroit, I didn't get close to too many horses. Where'd you say you were from?"

"Texas."

"I knew it!" Richie said. "I knew by your accent it had to be the southwest. I enjoy accents — trying to figure out where people come from. Of course, in the theater, everybody tries to get rid of their accents."

"Uh-huh," Toby said again. "Listen, like

I said, I'm mighty uncomfortable up here. Thanks for the tour, but could we go back down now?"

"Oh, sure," he said. "Sorry about that. Just follow me."

The catwalk was T-shaped, and Toby carefully inched her way along one of its arms, following Richie to the center stem, which would lead them to the light booth. Once she had something solid underneath her, she could listen to him some more and maybe find out if he was the mystery man. But for now, all she could concentrate on was reaching the light booth.

When they were halfway there, Richie stopped to adjust another light. "How you doing?" he asked.

"Not too bad," Toby said. "I think I'll make it."

"Just hang in there," he told her. Finishing with the light, he moved on, still talking a mile a minute.

"I shouldn't have brought you up here," he said over his shoulder. "Or I should have asked first if heights bothered you."

"That's okay," Toby said. "I didn't tell you." Dummy that I am, she thought.

"No need to be embarrassed, though," he said. "Everybody's got something they're scared of. With me, it's water. I don't mean I'm so terrified of it that I won't swim, but I'm never quite comfortable in water that's over my head. Anyway," he went on, "you're just like my fiancée. She can't stand heights either."

"Fiancée?" Toby finally asked. "I thought you went to Oakley. I mean, are you really engaged?"

Richie laughed, opened the door to the light-booth and jumped in off the catwalk. "I'm really engaged," he said, as Toby gratefully stepped in after him. "And I don't go to Oakley. I said I was *at* Oakley." He smiled at the look on her face. "I go to college. I'm on a work-study program, and this semester, I'm working. I'm an instructor at Oakley."

"There I was," Toby said to Jane that night, "hoping that I'd get down from there in one piece, and he turns out to be engaged." She stretched out on her bed and stared up at the tea bag. "He just talked so much that I missed the difference between going to Oakley and *being* at Oakley."

Jane smothered a smile. "You should be proud," she said solemnly. "You risked your life for a good cause. You're a true Canby Hall girl."

"I'm a true dummy, that's what I am," Toby said, laughing at last. "Not only that, I'm an empty-handed one. I didn't find Andy's admirer."

"I haven't done any better," Jane admitted. "But we can't give up. Not yet."

"I'm not about to give up," Toby said. She slid off the bed and picked up Jane's list. "We haven't tried the library yet. Maybe we'll hit paydirt there." She grinned at Jane. "One thing for sure, at least there's nothing to fall off of in the library."

CHAPTER TWELVE

The Canby Hall library was big and busy, so Toby and Jane decided to stake it out together. It would be Saturday before they could both find enough time, which was just as well, Jane pointed out. The library was at its busiest on the weekend, and there would be more of a chance that their note writer would show up then.

"We both have studying to do," she told Toby, "so we'll just do it at the library. That way we can keep an eye on everyone who comes and goes."

It was Thursday night, and the two of them were downstairs in Baker Hall, in the room with the vending machines, where they were using the long table to make posters for the Winter Festival.

"Maybe Andy will be there," Toby said, using a red marker to draw a slightly lop-sided sled. "It would sure be a lot easier if we could see somebody watching her like a lovesick calf. That would be a real good clue."

"It would be a giveaway," Jane agreed, her marker squeaking as she printed four-inch high letters on a poster. "But I wouldn't count on Andy coming to the library. She said something about a rehearsal tomorrow, among other things."

"Among *many* other things, I bet," Toby laughed.

"There you are!" a lilting southern-accented voice rang out, and Penny came in, followed by Dee and Maggie. "We've been searching up and down this entire dorm trying to find you two!"

"You've been holding out on us," Dee said accusingly. "Don't try to deny it."

"Okay," Toby said cheerfully. "We won't deny it. But do you mind telling us what it is?"

"You know!" Penny was at her most dramatic. "Did you really think we wouldn't find out?"

"About what?" Jane couldn't imagine what she and Toby had done, but it sounded extremely serious.

"About the box!" Maggie cried. "Andy's care package? She took it upstairs and you didn't even tell us!"

With a relieved smile, Jane turned to Toby, and they both burst out laughing. "Guilty as charged," Toby said. "But I don't think you'll be so mad when you find out exactly where Andy put that box."

"We'll be the judges of that," Dee said. "Where did she put it?"

"Under her bed," Toby said.

"Unopened," Jane added.

The others looked at each other.

"Now who feels guilty?" Jane asked.

Penny immediately spoke up. "On behalf of all of us, I apologize," she said contritely. "We should have known you wouldn't keep something like that to yourselves."

"She really hasn't opened it?" Maggie asked.

"She hasn't even looked at it since she brought it up to 407," Toby said. "It's sitting there gathering dust."

"Not under Andy's bed," Jane reminded her.

"Right. It's sitting there staying clean," Toby said.

"Such a waste," Penny said, shaking her head sadly.

During a moment of silence in which they all mourned the unopened care package, Andy walked in. "Oh, these look great!" she said, seeing the half-finished posters. She gave them a bright smile and bustled over to a vending machine. "And so do these. I'm starving."

The others watched, still quiet, as Andy put in her money and pulled the lever for a Baby Ruth. "Oh, by the way," she laughed, peeling back the wrapper, "I got another

one of those notes." She fished in the pocket
of her robe and took it out. "Listen to this
one: 'You haven't been in, and I think I
know why. If you don't come again, I surely
won't die — but I'll sigh.' "

With another laugh and a shake of her
head, Andy said she had to get back to the
study room, and walked out.

"I had one of those Baby Ruth's last
night," Penny remarked. "It was so old and
stale I thought I'd lose every tooth in my
mouth on it."

"Maybe she's saving the care package for
a rainy day," Maggie suggested.

"We won't have a rainy day until spring,"
Dee told her. "By then, whatever's in that
package will be as dried up and shriveled
as prunes."

"Maybe that's it!" Penny cried. "Her folks
sent her prunes. That's why she's not opening it."

Jane and Toby laughed along with the
others, but they had something else on their
minds besides the care package. The secret
admirer was unhappy because Andy hadn't
been in. And where hadn't she been in a
while? The Canby Hall library.

The library opened at eight-thirty on Saturday mornings. At eight forty-five, Toby
and Jane climbed the steps and went
through the big front doors.

"I hope we're right about this." Jane tried

to swallow a yawn and failed. "If we're not, I'll have lost three good hours of sleep for nothing."

"I'm not crazy about missing my walk, either," Toby said. She was wide awake and full of energy, and the idea of spending the entire day indoors was already giving her cabin fever. "But, like they say back home, if you're gonna tangle with a mule, you've gotta be willin' to swallow a powerful lot of dust."

Jane gave her a sleepy-eyed, skeptical look. "They don't really say that, do they?"

Toby grinned and shook her head. "I just made it up."

Jane had been right about one thing — the library was busy. From about nine o'clock on, the two roommates, who had stationed themselves at separate tables near the checkout desk, hardly got any of their own studying done. So many people were coming in and out that they didn't dare take their eyes from the door for fear they might miss the one person they were looking for. Most of the students were girls, fortunately, but there were plenty of boys from Oakley Prep and from the town itself.

Their plan was simple: whenever they spotted a likely candidate, they would take turns asking him a series of "survey" questions that they'd come up with the night before. Whoever wasn't asking the questions would keep her eyes out for the next questionee.

By noon, they'd interviewed fifteen boys.

Of the last two, one asked Toby for a date before she even got to the second survey question. She figured that anybody who was pining for Andy wouldn't be so quick to look at another girl. And the fifteenth told Jane that he'd never been in anyplace as full of snow and stuffy people as Massachusetts, and he couldn't wait to get home to Florida.

"Florida?" sniffed Jane, whose ancestors could be traced back to Plymouth Rock. "What exactly does Florida have besides alligators and swamps?"

"Warm sand and hot sun," the boy replied.

"Massachusetts has those, too," Jane had informed him.

"Sure it does," he sneered. "For all of two weeks out of the year."

"He's out," Jane reported to Toby, still indignant about his remarks. "He wouldn't look at a girl unless she had sand in her shoes and seaweed in her hair."

Toby laughed. "Not everybody loves this state, you know."

"I suppose not," Jane agreed reluctantly. "But not everybody's rude about it, either. Anyway," she went on, "it's time for lunch and I'm starved. I didn't think solving a mystery would give me such an appetite."

Jane went to lunch first, then relieved Toby. By one, they were both on duty again. By two, the stream of students had started to taper off. Most people had finished their work and were getting ready to enjoy their weekend. Or else they were sick of the library and had to get out no matter how much more studying they had to do. As of four o'clock, Jane and Toby had talked to only four more boys, none of whom were the one they were looking for.

"What do you think we should do?" Toby asked, taking a break from her own work. "This place closes at five."

Jane nodded. "I know," she sighed. "I suppose we might as well stay until the bitter end. Do you mind?"

"One more hour won't hurt," Toby said with a shrug. "Besides, I'm actually getting all my homework done and I'll have tomorrow free."

"So am I," Jane said. "Maybe we should do this more often. On the other hand," she added, seeing the look on Toby's face, "maybe we shouldn't."

It was four-thirty when he came in. Toby spotted him first, pushing hurriedly through the big front door, his red down jacket unzipped even though it was twenty degrees outside and getting colder fast. He stood by the checkout desk for a moment, glancing all around him, his eyes skimming over faces as if he were searching for one in particular. Maybe Andy's face, Toby thought excitedly.

His glance reached Toby, who was staring at him hard, a curious, expectant look on her face. He stared back, then looked away quickly and started for the bookshelves.

Toby reached for the pad of survey questions and remembered that Jane had it. She dashed over to Jane's table, whispered "This could be it," grabbed the pad, and turned around. The guy was gone.

Jane was on her feet. "Red jacket?"

Toby nodded. "Did he go outside?"

"No. Into the stacks," Jane said "DOP-DRI. I'll wait here in case he comes back to the desk before you find him."

Clutching the notepad, Toby strode across the floor and into the DOP-DRI row. It was empty. She walked to the end and then peered down the two rows on either side of it. Nobody.

When she came back out, Jane was waving wildly from her table. "He went that way," she reported when Toby reached her, and pointed toward the back of the big room where periodicals were kept.

Toby headed swiftly for the back. There were still several people there, mostly townspeople, sitting in the comfortable chairs reading magazines and newspapers. Behind the chairs were tall, uncurtained windows overlooking a stretch of snow-covered lawn.

It was getting dark outside, and reflected in the glass, Toby saw a figure in red crossing the floor behind her. She spun around just in time to see the quarry disappear into a row of books again.

Unaware that Toby had seen him, Jane left her post and went after him. There he was, at the end of the MOE-MOO row! Jane cleared her throat, and when he looked at her, she put on a businesslike smile and started toward him. "Excuse me," she called out in a stage whisper, "I wonder . . ."

Without a word, he stepped around the shelves and was out of sight. Jane hurried after him, turned the corner and almost collided with Toby.

"Where'd he go?"

"I don't know," Jane said breathlessly. "He was right in that very spot just a second ago!"

"Slippery critter," Toby muttered, and the two of them headed off in opposite directions.

The chase continued for almost another half hour, through the stacks, into the computer room, the map room, up the stairs to the vast research section and in and out of the various study and meeting rooms.

They both saw him several times, but each time they got close, he zipped around a corner or through a row of books before they could reach him.

"He knows we're trying to talk to him,"

Jane said as she and Toby crossed paths. "Why doesn't he stop?"

"Beats me," Toby said. "But he looks mighty secretive — like he's trying to hide something."

"The rare books!" Jane cried.

"What?"

"You know. Canby Hall library has a rare-books collection," Jane reminded her. "Forget about whether he's the secret admirer or not. He could be a thief!"

Toby's green eyes widened. "And we've been tailing him since he came in. He probably thinks we're out to get him."

"We are," Jane said. She straightened her shoulders and raised her chin. "Those books are worth a fortune. Come on!"

The two roommates hurried downstairs and past the stacks until they were just outside the room that housed the rare books.

Jane took a deep breath and peered around the edge of the door. She drew her head back and smiled grimly at Toby. "He's there," she whispered.

Toby nodded. "On three," she whispered back.

At the count, the two sleuths walked into the room and confronted the red-jacketed kid, who spun away from a shelf of leather-bound books, a plastic shopping bag clutched close to his chest.

"This is outrageous," Jane said in a

clipped voice. "You should be utterly ashamed of yourself."

Toby couldn't help smiling a little. Only Jane would try to shame a thief. "If you put the book back now," she said, "maybe the librarian won't be too hard on you. *Maybe*," she repeated.

The boy glanced around the room, confusion in his eyes. "Book?" he stammered. "What book?"

"There's no point in trying to deny it," Jane said. "We're talking about the book you've got in that bag."

The confused look disappeared, and he actually smiled. "In here?" he asked, holding out the bag. "You think I've got a book in here?"

"I hardly think it's a burger and fries," Jane told him.

His smile got wider. "Close," he said. "But not quite on target. Here. Take a look." He tossed over the bag, which landed at Toby's feet with a soft, un-booklike plop.

Toby picked up the bag and looked inside. First she blushed, then she grinned. Then she laughed out loud. "You'll never guess," she said to Jane.

"I'm not in the mood for guessing," Jane said, feeling a blush of her own start to creep up her neck. Obviously she and Toby had committed an extremely embarrassing blunder. "Just tell me."

"Doughnuts," Toby reported, and laughed even louder.

"It was a scavenger hunt," the boy explained, enjoying himself now. "The clue was 'Hall of learning, row after row, until you find the stacks of dough.' Guessing the library was easy," he went on, "but I thought the dough meant money. I thought for sure I'd find a stack of bills somewhere in here."

Jane's blush had reached her face now, and she kept quiet.

"But why did you run away from us?" Toby asked.

"I thought you were on the hunt, too. It's a contest, you know." he said. "I thought you were following me, and I didn't want to give you any clues."

"We're not on the hunt," Toby said. "Sorry about chasing you all over. I guess we sort of jumped to the wrong conclusion."

"That's okay," he told them. Then he looked confused again. "But how about telling me just why you *were* following me."

"Of course." Jane had recovered her poise by now. Smiling calmly, she flipped open her notepad. "We're conducting a survey. Would you mind answering a few questions?"

CHAPTER THIRTEEN

"I have to hand it to you," Toby said to Jane as they left the library and started back to Baker House. "You don't give up. I could tell you were ready to die of embarrassment, but that didn't stop you."

Jane laughed, her breath making white puffs in the frosty air. "Well, once we discovered he wasn't a thief, I thought we might as well find out what he really was, besides a scavenger, I mean."

"The look on his face!" Toby hooted. "Did you ever see anybody so confounded in his life?"

"I'm sure he thought we were crazy," Jane agreed. "But he covered it up very well. The only thing that gave him away was how he kept inching toward the door every time I asked him a question." She giggled. "I guess he thought if he just stayed calm, maybe we wouldn't go completely bananas on him." She thought about it a minute. "Actually, he was very nice. Nice-looking, too."

"Yep."

"I liked him."

"Me, too."

As Jane pointed out, even though the boy obviously wanted nothing more than to escape the two girls who'd been chasing him through the library for half an hour, he did answer her survey questions. And before he finally fled in relief, it was clear that he wasn't Andy's mysterious admirer any more than he was a rare-book thief.

"What now?" Toby wondered as they went into the dorm and started upstairs to 407.

"Tomorrow we'll try to think of another plan," Jane said. "Right now, all I want is a shower, then dinner, and some time with Cary." She cringed slightly as she thought of something. "Wait until he hears about what happened today. He'll never let us forget it!"

Jane was right about that. Cary thought the big stake-out at the library was the funniest story he'd heard in years; he immediately dubbed Toby and Jane the "Sleuth Sisters," and suggested they take out an ad in the yellow pages under the heading for comedy acts. Jane was not as amused as he was and told him that he'd eat his words one day.

"We've already covered all the places she

goes," Toby said after lunch on Sunday. "I suppose we could do it again — after all, we probably missed him. But it was a long shot in the first place, and it's not going to get any better."

"This is so frustrating," Jane sighed. "You'd think he'd *want* her to know who he is. But his notes aren't exactly filled with clues."

"Just that last one about how she hasn't been in for a while." Toby was getting ready to go outside for some air and she thought a minute while she tugged on her boots. "You know, maybe we should just come right out and ask Andy who she thinks it is."

"I doubt if she's given it more than two seconds' thought," Jane said. "I suppose it won't hurt to try, though."

But when they asked, Andy just laughed. "Who knows?" she said. "It's probably just a joke."

Toby and Jane didn't think it was a joke. It had gone on too long, for one thing. For another, a sixth note arrived sometime during Sunday afternoon. This one was short and sweet: "No time to rhyme. Hope to see you sometime. (Hey, it *did* rhyme!)"

The thing that bothered Jane and Toby most was that the writer might give up before they found him. True, he seemed awfully persistent, as Jane said, but nobody could bounce off a stone wall forever.

Unfortunately, when Monday rolled around, they still hadn't decided on what to do next, and now that they were back in the routine of classes, they didn't have as much time. Plus, Wednesday was the day of the Winter Festival. When they weren't in class, or trying to study, eat, or sleep, Andy kept reminding them to put up posters all over the place. They did, but they only put them up around Canby Hall, which didn't satisfy Andy. "The Greenleaf High School's carnival is open to the whole town," she said. "Ours should be, too, don't you think?"

Jane and Toby took the hint, and Cary was loaded up with several posters for Oakley Prep. Toby volunteered to cover one area of Greenleaf, and Jane took another. Toby got hers up right away, but Jane kept putting it off and Andy finally got fed up.

"All you have to do is tape a few posters to a few store windows," she said Monday night. "I don't see what the big deal is."

"It's not a big deal," Jane said. "I've just been busy."

"With what?" Andy looked skeptical. "Your side of the room's a mess, as usual, so you haven't been busy with that."

Jane's chin came up and Toby, who was writing a letter to her father and Emma, knew she was mad.

"I do have studying to do," Jane said

coolly. "And I also like to enjoy myself. Not everyone wants to keep so busy they don't have time for life."

"What does that mean?" Andy asked.

"You know," Jane said. "It means you don't have fun anymore. It also means you *aren't* fun anymore."

Andy seemed to ignore Jane's second comment. "I really don't understand," she said. "But if you're too busy having fun, then give me the posters and *I'll* put them up."

"Oh, no you won't!" Jane rolled up the posters, snapped a rubber band around them, and shoved them under her bed. "I made them and I'll put them up." She went to her desk and picked up her history book. "When I have time," she added over her shoulder.

It was late Tuesday afternoon before Jane finally got around to pulling the posters out from under her bed. At least she could be sure that Andy didn't know she'd taken this long. Andy never came near the underside of Jane's bed for fear of being choked by dust curls.

Still, Jane felt guilty as she took out the roll of papers and blew off the dust. There was always the chance that Andy might come along, see what she was up to, and start tapping her foot. She did a lot of foot-tapping lately, Jane had noticed, and if she did it one more time, there just might be problems. So Jane hid the posters as well as she could underneath her soft camel-hair jacket and left the room, hoping to make a clean, unnoticed getaway.

Glancing up and down the hall, Jane raced for the stairs. She was at the top of the last staircase, looking down to the main hall, when she noticed a boy standing just inside the door. There was still an hour before dinner, and most girls were either in their rooms or away, at the library or the skating pond or the Greaf. Anyway, the main hall was empty. Except for the boy.

It was shadowy in the hall, so Jane couldn't see his face very well, but light from the big crystal lamp overhead shone on his hands, one of which was reaching into the pocket of his bright blue jacket. As Jane watched, he pulled out a folded piece of white paper.

Jane's right foot was still poised in the air, ready to step down, and now she held it there, not moving a muscle. Because she knew. The minute she saw that piece of paper, she knew she was looking at Andy's secret admirer.

Trying to breathe as quietly as possible, hoping he wouldn't glance up, Jane saw the boy move swiftly from the door to the long, shining table at the side of the hall. He dropped the paper onto the table and tapped it once with his finger. Then, without looking back, he crossed to the door and let himself out into the winter twilight.

Then Jane moved. Clinging to the banister with one hand, she almost flew down the stairs, then skidded over the polished tiles, bumped against the table and snatched up the note. "Dear Andy," was all she needed to read before she threw the note back on the table and ran outside.

There he was, walking quickly across the common toward the main street of Greenleaf, his blue jacket easy to spot as he weaved his way through groups of students returning to the dorm. I've got him! Jane thought excitedly.

At the end of the common, he took a right turn. Still clutching the posters under her jacket, Jane did the same. All she had to do, she thought, was follow him wherever he went and then . . . well, she wasn't sure what she'd do then. It depended on where he was going. It could be the Greaf or Oakley Prep. Both of them were in this direction.

Oakley would be easy. She'd just see which dorm he went into, tell Cary about it, and have him find out who he was. The Greaf would be tricky. Now that she knew for sure that he was the note-writer, she didn't think she could keep a straight face and ask her survey questions.

But it didn't matter. She'd think of something. Now that she'd found him, she wasn't about to let him get away.

After five minutes of brisk walking, the boy reached the Greaf. And passed it. Twenty feet behind him, Jane breathed a sigh of relief. She had her fingers crossed for Oakley Prep.

But when the boy reached the street that would have led him toward the boys' school, he walked on by.

All right, Jane thought. He must be going somewhere else. The Greenleaf Inn wasn't far, maybe he planned to eat dinner there. That would be a little surprising, considering how expensive it was, but it was still possible. And it would show that he had good taste. Better yet, maybe he worked there. Then *she* could enjoy a great meal and find out who he was at the same time.

The Greenleaf Inn came and went. The boy kept walking and so did Jane. He can't go far, Jane kept telling herself. Greenleaf's not that big. It doesn't take more than fifteen minutes to get from Canby Hall to anywhere in town.

Of course, it was possible that he was just taking a walk. Jane hoped not. She wasn't in the mood for trailing him around town while he stretched his legs.

Finally, shortly after he'd passed the Inn, the boy slowed down in front of a building. Jane came to a stop and watched as he went inside. Then she hurried up the sidewalk until she was standing in front of the Greenleaf Library.

It's too bad Toby's not here, Jane thought with a smile. What's another library stake-out with the second Sleuth Sister along to help? Jane hurried up the steps and into the library.

As it turned out, she didn't need to hurry. Once Jane was inside the door, she saw him. Still wearing the jacket, he walked to the end of the main desk, and then went around behind it. He took off his jacket and hung it from a peg on the wall. He exchanged a smile and a few words with the woman who was stamping out books, then took hold of something and pushed. When he was out from behind the desk, Jane saw that he was pushing a loaded bookcart.

Now she could see him perfectly. He was medium height, with a nice athletic build; his black hair was cut very short. He wore jeans and a deep purple cotton sweater. He was handsome. He had a nice smile. He was also, Jane realized, the "creep" from the Greenleaf Library.

Ten minutes went by while Jane tried to decide what to do. She took one minute to tack one of her posters to the bulletin board along with all the other notices. Then she went back to thinking.

Andy had talked about this boy as if he were an enemy. Jane had gotten the impression that he was rude and crude and completely unfeeling.

But he was the secret admirer. Jane knew that. How could such a rude, unfeeling person write such funny, caring little poems?

It was a completely new mystery, and Jane decided there was only one way to solve it. She straightened her shoulders, tossed back her hair, and walked down a row of books until she was standing next to the bookcart.

The boy was shelving books and didn't notice her. She cleared her throat and said, "I enjoyed your poems. They're not the best I've ever read, but I think they were the nicest."

A book fell to the floor as he turned around to face her, a hopeful look in his eyes. When he saw that she wasn't Andy, the look changed to embarrassment and maybe even anger.

Jane smiled, to show that she wasn't teasing or laughing at him. "My name's Jane Barrett," she said. "I'm Andy Cord's roommate. Would you mind if I asked you a few questions?"

CHAPTER FOURTEEN

A few minutes later, Jane and the "creep" were sitting at a low table in the children's section of the library. It was almost empty, and they were far enough away from the other sections so they could talk without having to whisper. Jane had finally learned his name, which was Todd Williams, and that he went to the Greenleaf High School. Now she was waiting to learn more.

"Sending unsigned notes isn't exactly the way I usually try to get a know a girl," Todd said, smiling at himself as much as at Jane. "In fact, I was all set to walk right up and ask Andy for a date."

"Why didn't you?"

"For one thing, she stopped coming in for a while," he said. "Not that she was here that often, but after I'd finally gotten up my courage and decided to invite her out, I didn't see her at all for a long time."

That must have been when we went to

Montavia, Jane thought, deciding not to mention Ramad. "We took a trip," she told him. "Toby — that's our other roommate — and Andy and I."

"I thought it must be something like that," Todd said. "Anyway, when she finally came back, I decided not to waste any time, in case she went away again." He shook his head and shifted around in the small, child-sized chair. "But I changed my mind. She just didn't seem the same. I got the real strong feeling that if I asked her for a date, she'd either pretend not to hear me or else she'd chew me out."

Jane laughed. She didn't know Todd Williams very well yet, but she was sure of one thing — he was pretty fast when it came to figuring Andy out. "So you started writing poetry," she commented.

"Bad poetry," he said with a grin. "Like I said, that's not my usual style, but the way Andy was acting, I thought I needed to try something different. When I found her glove, I was just going to send it back, but then I thought I'd write a note with it, and my first great poem just popped into my head!" He shifted in his chair again and smiled. "The poems turned out to be fun and I was hoping she'd think so, too. It seemed like that's what was missing when she came back — fun."

"The poems *were* fun," Jane told him. "But they didn't tell her much. I mean, how long were you going to keep her guessing?"

Todd laughed. "I never expected to write so many," he said. "I was going to send her a couple of them and then let her know it was me. But I got another strong feeling — that she couldn't have cared less *who* it was."

Jane was quiet, not sure what to say. If she was completely honest, she'd have to tell him he was right. Andy couldn't have cared less. But if she told him that, he might give up. And Jane didn't want him to do that. Because she'd learned something else about Todd Williams — he was no creep. In fact, if Andy only had her head on straight, she'd probably agree that he was one of the nicest guys in Greenleaf.

But why had Andy called him a creep? No matter what she said about falling in love again, she couldn't be totally blind, especially about somebody like Todd.

"Andy talked about you, by the way," Jane said now.

Todd's eyes lit up. "She did? No kidding?"

"She wanted to reserve a book here, and she mentioned that you weren't very . . . um . . ." Jane hesitated. How could she say it without insulting him? ". . . very helpful," she finished.

"Oh, that!" Todd laughed again, not insulted at all. "Yeah, that wasn't supposed to happen. But she just got me mad. In fact, she got me mad a couple of times." He shook his head, still smiling. "The funny thing was, I almost enjoyed it. At least she had some of her spark back."

That's exactly the way I felt about it, Jane thought. "You really like her, don't you?" she asked.

"I really do." Todd got up, his hands in his pockets, and walked a few paces away. He peered in the fish tank, which was burbling on a shelf underneath a Winnie The Pooh poster, and then turned back to Jane. "But I'm beginning to think it doesn't matter."

Jane couldn't blame him for thinking that, but she didn't want him to quit now. "I have a strong feeling, too," she said. "And that's if you and Andy could get together for a while, she just might decide she likes you, too. I can't guarantee it," she added quickly, "but I think it's worth a try."

"The creep at the library?" Toby said when Jane got back to 407. "I don't believe it!"

"It's true, though," Jane said happily, and told her everything she knew about Todd Williams. When she was finished, Toby agreed that he didn't seem at all like a creep. "Andy's got blinders on," she said. "She's just been staring straight ahead, that's her problem. She needs to look around."

"Well, she'll look around tomorrow," Jane told her. "I'll make sure of it."

"What's tomorrow? Oh, right, the festival," Toby said. "You mean he's coming?"

"Yes, and what we have to do is make sure she doesn't run around arranging things the whole time," Jane said. "Todd wants to talk to her, but he shouldn't have to tackle her first."

"Maybe I could lasso her," Toby joked.

"Don't laugh," Jane told her. "You just might have to."

They were still discussing how to get Andy to give Todd the time of day when Maggie, Dee, and Penny knocked on the door. "Help!" Penny said, "we need refuge!"

"Come on in," Toby told them. "You can always hide in here. Just crawl behind that pile of clothes on Jane's bed and nobody will find you for a month."

"Very funny," Jane said. "Since Andy doesn't bother to tease me about it anymore, I see you've decided to take her place."

"Wouldn't want you to feel ignored," Toby grinned at Jane and turned back to the others. "What are you hiding from, anyway?"

"Your other roommate," Maggie whispered.

"Uh-oh," Toby said. "What's the problem?"

"Same old thing," Dee said.

"She's just pestering us to death about tomorrow," Penny explained. "For once, I did everything I was supposed to do — got the supplies for the hot chocolate and bought gallons of cider — and I actually did it on time, too! But Andy keeps coming back to check, 'just to make sure,' she says."

"She's doing the same thing to Dee and me," Maggie told them. "And we're as ready as we can be. So we just thought we'd hide out in here for a while."

"What makes you think she won't find you here?" Jane asked. "This is her room, after all."

Penny laughed. "Because she told us she wanted to find you, to ask if you finally finished putting up those posters. And she was heading for the Greaf when she said it."

"This is terrible," Jane said, even though she couldn't help laughing, too. "We're actually hiding out from one of our best friends."

"It can't last much longer. Who knows?" Toby asked innocently. "By tomorrow, things might even be different."

"They might," Jane agreed. "But you better dig out your rope, just in case."

"What on earth are you talking about?" Penny wanted to know.

Jane and Toby exchanged glances. They hadn't told the others about their search for the anonymous poet, because they were afraid that if too many people found out, it might get back to Andy. And she wouldn't appreciate it one bit, they were sure of that.

But maybe they hadn't been fair, keeping it a secret. Dee and Maggie and Penny were

Andy's friends, too. And they cared about her as much as they griped about her.

"You have to promise not to breathe a word of this to anyone, especially Andy," Jane told them, after she and Toby had nodded at each other.

"This sounds serious," Maggie said.

"It is, but it's not bad," Toby told her. "Jane found him."

"Found who?" Dee asked.

"I know!" Penny cried excitedly. "Andy's secret admirer!"

"Right," Jane said, and told them all about it. "Tomorrow, if everything goes according to plan, Andy's going to find out who he is, too. It might not work out, of course, but if she gives him half a chance, we just might see a different Andy around here." She smiled and held up her hand. "So keep your fingers crossed for tomorrow."

Jane woke up on Wednesday morning earlier than usual, and the first thing she saw was Andy, standing at the window and staring outside. She stood very still, which was a change, and Jane could tell by the way her shoulders slumped that she wasn't full of her usual energy.

Just wait, Jane thought. In a few hours, everything might be different.

Yawning and stretching, Jane punched up her pillow and got into a sitting position. Her clock said seven, so she knew she must be getting excited about getting Andy and Todd together. Worry and excitement were about the only two things that could make her give up sleep, especially on a day when classes were canceled. Even Toby was still asleep.

Andy still hadn't moved. "Is something happening outside?" Jane asked, yawning again.

Finally, Andy sighed. "You might say that."

"Well, what?" Jane sat up straighter and reached for her hairbrush. "More snow?"

Andy made a funny noise, sort of a cross between a hiccup and a sniff. "I just don't believe it," she said.

"Good grief, what is it?" Jane asked again. She threw off the covers and joined Andy at the window. "Whatever it is, I hope it's — " Jane broke off as she took her first look out the window.

It seemed impossible, but it was true: the snow was gone. Well, not completely. There *were* still piles of it where it had been shoveled, piles that seemed to be getting smaller by the minute. And there were patches of it all across the common, but Jane could see brown grass poking through them. In fact, the entire common looked like a swamp.

"I don't believe it, either," Jane said finally. "But it does happen sometimes. By next week, it'll probably be a winter wonderland again."

"Probably," Andy agreed. "But next week will be too late. Today's the Winter Festival." She shook her head and sighed again. "Whoever heard of a winter festival without snow?"

Jane was upset, too, but not for quite the same reason Andy was. They'd worked hard for this day, and it was too bad the weather hadn't decided to cooperate. Once everyone saw what kind of day it was, they'd pack up their sleds and iceskates. They might even dig out their bathing suits. No one would come to the Winter Festival, including Todd Williams. And to Jane, that was the most disappointing thing about this sudden thaw.

Across the room, Toby stirred and threw back her rainbow comforter. "Mornin'," she said, rubbing her eyes with the heels of her hands. She blinked a few times and finally noticed that her two roommates hadn't stopped looking out the window. "What's up?"

"The temperature," Andy snapped, and stalked off to take a shower.

Toby climbed out of bed and joined Jane at the window. "No wonder Andy went off in a huff," she commented. "No festival, that's for sure."

"And no rendezvous, either," Jane reminded her. "We'll have to figure out another way to get them together."

It was Todd who came up with another meeting place. Like everyone else, he knew there wouldn't be any festival that day, but he went to Canby Hall after school anyway, and called for Jane. Toby was with her when he came, and the three of them went to the Greaf together, discussing the situation on the way.

"It's no problem," Todd said after a few minutes. "Why don't all of you just come to the Winter Carnival at Greenleaf High on Saturday? There'll be lots of people, and I can just 'run in' to Andy like I was going to do today."

"That might be all right," Jane said doubtfully. "But what if this warm spell lasts and that carnival is canceled, too?"

"No chance," Todd told her. "Ours is indoors. It's just like all the other school carnivals — games and bake sales and stuff. We just call it the Winter Carnival because we always have it around this time."

Toby laughed. "You know, Andy got her idea for the Canby Hall carnival after she saw the high school's poster. I guess she didn't read it very carefully."

Toby liked Todd immediately. He didn't talk too much, and when he did, he said what was on his mind. He had a sense of humor, too, but most important, he really seemed to care about Andy.

"Well, well, if it isn't the Sleuth Sisters!" Cary remarked as they walked into the diner. He hadn't noticed that Todd was with them, and his eyes were twinkling as he led them to a booth. "What's the mystery today, may I ask? A purloined pizza, perhaps?"

Jane gave him a triumphant smile, and then turned to Todd, who was standing slightly behind Cary. "Todd, this is Cary Slade. He thinks he's very amusing, so we humor him because we like him so much." She put her hand on Cary's arm and gestured toward Todd. "Cary, this is Todd Williams. He likes to write short poems. And we like him, especially because he *admires* Andy so much."

Cary, for once, was silent.

"You better close your mouth," Toby told him. "It's warm enough for flies today, and one of them just might buzz right in there."

"Don't worry, we won't let that happen!" Jane assured him. She was busy writing something on her napkin, and when she finished, she held it out to him. "I told you you'd eat your words one day," she said with a gleam in her eye. "So start chewing!"

CHAPTER FIFTEEN

The Greenleaf High School's Winter Carnival was on Saturday, and it was the perfect place for the rendezvous, but it took Jane and Toby all of Thursday and most of Friday to talk Andy into going. Her first reaction was, "I don't want to hear the words *winter carnival* for at least five years, maybe even more."

"Come on," Toby said. "It wasn't your fault the weather changed and we couldn't have the Canby Hall Winter Festival."

"Ha," Andy retorted. "Try telling P.A. that. Everytime she sees me she shakes her head and clicks her tongue at me. I feel like I ought to go into hiding."

Andy's next excuse was that she was too busy. Jane was ready for that one. "You already finished that paper you were working on," she pointed out. "We were off on Wednesday, so you won't have as much homework, and you can do it on Sunday.

Or Friday night, if you really want to be disgusting about it. And," she added, "there aren't any dance rehearsals this weekend. I checked."

Andy finally stopped making up excuses and admitted that she simply didn't want to go. "I'm just not in the mood," was how she put it.

"Not in the mood for fun?" Toby remarked to the tea bag on the ceiling. "That's weird. The Andy Cord I know is always ready for fun."

Andy didn't comment, but when they got up on Saturday morning, she finally agreed to go. "It might be interesting," she said as she got dressed. "I've never been in the high school. I don't even think I know a single person from there."

Jane and Toby didn't say a word, but they shared a secret smile, and went to get Penny, Maggie, and Dee to join the group from 407.

"Did Todd tell you where he'd be?" Toby whispered softly to Jane as they walked up the steps to the high schol after lunch.

Jane shook her head. "I forgot to ask," she whispered back. "But don't worry. He'll find Andy, we can be sure of that."

The school was packed with people. Every hall and room on the first floor was filled with booths — for darts, a fortune teller, a ring toss, picture-taking, popcorn, and just about anything else a carnival could have. Penny and Dee and Maggie got caught up in the spirit of it immediately, and stopped at almost every booth. Andy wandered off on her own, just looking, while Jane and Toby trailed behind her, hoping to see what happened when she met up with Todd.

Toby spotted Todd first. He was working in a booth, selling Greenleaf High School sweatshirts, which were bright green with gold lettering. Poking Jane in the side, she pointed to Andy, who had seen the sweatshirts and was making her way over to the booth. "Looks like she's interested," Toby said.

"She can never resist adding to her sweatshirt collection," Jane agreed.

The two of them dropped back a few more feet, and then Toby suggested, "Maybe we should make ourselves scarce."

"You're right," Jane said. "I'd love to eavesdrop, but this is really between them. I guess we'll have to keep our fingers crossed and wait."

Jane and Toby were right about Andy and the sweatshirts. She bought one almost everywhere she went, and besides, she really liked this color combination. A lot of other kids were buying them, so she had to wait, but finally she reached the edge of the table.

"You look like a medium," a voice said.

"I want a large, though," Andy said without looking up. "They always shrink and then they're not comfortable."

"I'm supposed to tell you they run true to size and refuse to shrink even when threatened," the voice said. "But I won't."

Andy glanced up then, smiling. When she saw who belonged to the voice, the smile disappeared. "Oh," she said. "It's you."

Todd held out his hands and grinned. "Look — I'm not pushing a bookcart, so I can't run you down."

"Is that supposed to be good news?" Andy asked.

"Sure. You're not in any danger," Todd said. "That's good, isn't it?"

Andy dropped the sweatshirt she was holding and walked away. But Todd, after a quick word to the other boy who was selling, sped out from behind the table, caught up to her, and started walking along with her.

"So," he said casually, "what do you think of Greenleaf High?"

"Is that your other job?" Andy asked. "Tour guide?"

"No, but if you're interested, I'd be happy to show you around."

Andy took a deep breath. "I'm not interested," she said. "I was being sarcastic." She snuck a look at him and discovered he was still smiling. Was he really enjoying this? "What's so amusing?" she asked.

"I was just wondering how long you intended to hold a grudge against me," he told her. "You don't seem the grudge-holding type. You don't really think I meant to hit you with the bookcart, do you?"

"It wasn't the bookcart," Andy said. She really didn't want to talk to this boy, but as long as he insisted, she decided to give him a piece of her mind. "It was the way you acted. I was trying to get to the desk to reserve a book for a paper I had to do, and you kept making smart remarks for so long that I never made it."

"Oh, so that's it." Todd thought a minute. "Tell me something. Did you get the paper done?"

"Yes."

"Did you get a good grade?"

"I don't know. It's not due for ten days."

Todd whistled. "Boy, you're really something. I don't think I've ever finished a paper more than a day ahead of time."

"Well, I usually don't either, but . . ." Andy broke off. Very tricky. He'd almost made her jump into a conversation with him.

"Tell me something," he said again. "How'd you get the paper done if you didn't have that book?"

Andy took another deep breath. "I got it done because somebody — somebody nice and thoughtful — found my notebook and sent it to my dorm." There, she thought.

That's absolutely the last thing I'm going to say to him.

"That *was* nice and thoughtful," he agreed. "And you don't know who it was?"

Andy shook her head.

"Whoever it was didn't even write a little note?"

Andy nodded.

"But it wasn't signed, huh?" Todd pretended to look confused. "I know. Why don't you tell me what the note said? There might be a clue in it."

Andy rolled her eyes.

"Oh, come on," Todd urged. "I like mysteries. Why don't you tell me? No, wait! Let me guess." He frowned in pretended concentration, and then he said, " 'I was glancing around, and look what I found. When you get it you'll smile, I hope for a while.' "

Andy stopped walking. It was the poem she'd found on the floor when she came back from the study room the night her notebook had been returned. How could he. . . ? Slowly, Andy turned her head and looked at him.

Todd was smiling "Was I close?" he asked.

It was almost an hour later, and Andy was still wandering by herself around the halls of the high school. Jane and Toby, Penny, Maggie, and Dee had all seen her, but she seemed so wrapped up in her thoughts that none of them wanted to bother her.

"Does anyone know if she met up with the mystery man?" Penny asked when the five of them had gathered in front of the popcorn booth.

Jane nodded. "I saw him a few minutes ago," she said. "He was too busy to talk, but he gave me a thumbs-up signal."

"Well, she didn't make a beeline for the door," Toby commented. "I guess that's a good sign."

"But she isn't exactly jumping up and down for joy, either," Dee remarked.

"We can't expect that," Jane said. "I just hope she gives him half a chance. I have the feeling that's all he needs."

Just then, they all spotted Andy down at the other end of the hall, walking slowly by herself.

"She doesn't look unhappy," Maggie observed. "She just looks confused."

Maggie was right. Andy *was* confused. Ever since she found out that the boy from the library was her secret note-writer, she'd been walking around in a fog. And what confused her the most was that she *hadn't* made a beeline for the door. Not because of the way he'd acted in the library — she really wasn't as mad about that anymore as she'd let him think.

This boy liked her, she thought. He'd returned her glove and her notebook, he'd come to see her dance, and he'd sent her half a dozen poems to prove it. But she didn't want any boy's attention, not after what happened with Ramad. So why hadn't she turned right around and headed back to Canby Hall?

There was a booth selling cans of soda up ahead; Andy walked over to it and bought a Coke. Then she moved on, sipping and thinking.

Why was she still here? Was there something about this guy that made her not leave? He was nice-looking, she'd give him that. Especially his eyes, with those long lashes. But he wasn't the first good-looking boy she'd ever seen, so it couldn't be that. What else was there about him?

He didn't give up, that was for sure. She'd been about as unfriendly as possible at the library, and almost rude to him today, and he didn't seem to mind. In fact, he acted like he enjoyed it.

That was weird, Andy thought. Imagine enjoying a fight. Of course, he didn't have much choice. If he liked her as much as those poems said he did, and he wanted to be with her, then he had to settle for arguments, because she hadn't given him anything else.

She hadn't given anyone much of anything else lately, she realized. Not that she'd been fighting with everybody. Most of the time, she'd kept herself too busy for that. But she knew she hadn't been the friendly, laughing Andy that she usually was. As Jane said, she just wasn't much fun. And when she'd slowed down for five minutes, she had to admit that most of what she did was either boss people around or argue with them. Jane would agree with that, she thought with a wry smile. And Toby probably would, too, even though she hadn't said anything.

But Jane and Toby were her best friends. Friends understood and stuck by you, even when you were bossy and argumentative and about as much fun as a toothache. Was that what this boy was doing? It must be. He really must think she was something special, to put up with all the guff she'd given him. And maybe that was it, she thought suddenly. Maybe she was still walking around this school thinking about him because the way he acted made her feel special, something she hadn't felt since Montavia.

Finishing her soda, Andy tossed the can in a trash barrel, spun on her heel, and marched quickly through the halls until she came to the sweatshirt booth. He was still there.

Andy made her way up to the table. "I wonder if you could tell me something," she said. "Two somethings."

He nodded. "I'll try."

"First, I wonder if you still have any sweatshirts left in size large."

He fumbled through the piles of shirts,

checking the labels, and finally pulled one out. "You're in luck," he told her, holding it up.

"I think you might be right," Andy said, taking it from him. "Now, the second thing," she went on. "I've been walking around for a while. And in my mind I've been calling you 'the guy,' and 'the boy,' and 'him.' " She stopped and smiled at him, a real Andy Cord smile. "I wonder if you could tell me your name?"

Todd smiled back, a mixture of relief and happiness in his eyes. "I thought you'd never ask," he said.

The next day was Sunday. Jane, as usual, slept late, and even Toby didn't rise at the crack of dawn. She did wake, but seeing that it was snowing and blowing again, she decided that her morning walk could wait a while. She rolled over on her back, stared at the tea bag, thought about her father and Emma, and was asleep again in five minutes.

The next thing Toby knew, someone was poking her in the arm. "I'm surprised at you, Toby Houston," Andy was saying. "Any self-respecting Texas ranch person would have been up with the chickens, and here it is, almost ten o'clock in the morning."

Toby pushed the quilt down and blinked. "We don't have a chicken ranch," she mumbled.

"That's a feeble excuse," Andy laughed.

A loud yawn came from Jane's bed. "What's all the noise?" she asked sleepily. Then she bolted upright. "Did I miss my first class?" she gasped.

Andy laughed again. "Relax. You don't have to worry about that until tomorrow."

"Oh, that's good." Jane flopped back down and was quiet for a minute. Then she lifted her head and looked at Andy. "You're up. And dressed. Have you really been outside already?"

"I just got back," Andy said happily. "I took a walk."

"That's my job," Toby commented. Then she sat up and took a closer look at Andy. "What's that you're wearing?" she asked, her eyes starting to sparkle.

"This?" Andy zipped her jacket down further. "It's my Greenleaf High School sweatshirt. I bought it yesterday."

Jane and Toby smiled at each other. "It looks good on you," Jane said. "Um . . . about that walk you just took. Did you take it alone?"

"Funny you should ask," Andy told her. "No, I didn't take it alone. I took it with a boy named Todd Williams."

"Nice name," Toby said innocently.

Jane swallowed a giggle and asked, "Who's Todd Williams?"

Andy grinned at them both and then burst out laughing again. "Come on, you two," she said. "You know who Todd Williams is. We didn't just walk together. We talked — about a lot of things."

Her two roommates exchanged a bigger smile.

"It's a good thing I didn't know what you were up to," Andy said. "I probably would have stopped you, and then where would I be?" She sat down on her bed, then jumped up again. "What I'm trying to say is thanks," she told them. "I'm starting to feel like Andy Cord again, and that feels good."

"It sounds good, too," Toby said.

"I don't have much time now," Andy went on. "But later, we can talk about everything. Especially Todd."

"What do you mean you don't have much time?" Jane asked. "That doesn't sound like the old Andy Cord. That sounds like the new one, the one who had fifteen projects going at the same time."

"Well, this isn't a project," Andy laughed. "But Todd and I didn't have breakfast, yet, and we're meeting at the Greaf in ten minutes. We still have a lot to talk about, and besides, I'm starving."

"It's the old Andy Cord, all right," Toby remarked.

"Wait a minute!" Jane called, as Andy headed for the door. "You admit that Toby and I had a hand in getting you and Todd together?"

"A hand?" Andy joked. "I'd say it was four hands, at least."

"And you're grateful?" Jane went on.

"I said thank you," Andy told her. "I guess that doesn't sound like much, but I meant it."

"We know you meant it, and it sounds fine," Jane said. "But as long as you're going off to the Greaf and leaving us to the mercy of the dining hall, there is one little thing you could do." She tilted her head in the direction of Andy's bed.

Toby laughed. "Right. Just one little thing."

"Sure." Andy looked confused. "Just tell me."

Throwing back her covers, Jane got up, went to Andy's bed, and dragged out the still-wrapped cardboard box. "This," she said, hefting it onto the bed. "You could open this and let us have some of it."

Andy laughed so hard it was almost a minute before she could speak. "I'll tell you what," she finally gasped. "I've got to get going, but you go ahead and open it. And take whatever you want." She left then, her laughter trailing behind her all the way down the hall.

Jane and Toby fell on the box, ripped off the brown paper, and pulled the flaps open. Then they stared.

Finally, Toby said, "Sheets?"

"Her family sent her sheets," Jane said slowly. "No wonder she thought it was so funny."

"No wonder she didn't open it."

Suddenly, they heard a muffled shout from outside, and running to the window, they saw Andy down on the common. She was waving to them, a big smile on her face. Jane and Toby waved back, laughing and smiling, too. After all, how could they be disappointed about a boxful of sheets when they had their roommate back?

Alison, former housemother at Canby Hall until she got married, has a big surprise for the roommates of 407, old and new — but does a new baby need six godmothers who can't agree on *anything*? Read Canby Hall #33, SIX ROOMMATES AND A BABY.